MW00879962

Amie Denman

Dedication

The Gull Motel is dedicated to my two sisters who live in Florida and always put out the welcome mat when I want to escape the cold weather in the Midwest. Thank you for your inspiration, information, friendship, and love.

Chapter One

Vacation. Despite my brainy reputation, this was one of the smartest things I'd done in a long time. When my middle school math teacher shortened my name from Savannah to Savvy, I took on a persona that drove me all the way through college at the top of my class. But now, I planned to put my brain on ice and my butt in the hot sand at my aunt and uncle's lovably shabby beachside Florida motel. It was the most savvy thing I could do while I played an endless waiting game with the job market.

It was a hot September morning when I rolled into the steaming lot at the Gull Motel. Everything about it said Old Florida. A miniature palm tree grew in a concrete planter in front of the *Office* sign. The few cars nosed up to numbered doors looked hot enough to combust. It wasn't a hotel, it didn't have the cachet. But it looked like a four-diamond resort to me as my burly Uncle Mike swung open the frosted glass office door and grinned at me like Santa had just landed on his roof.

"Your aunt's got the margarita machine going already," he said, crushing me in a massive hug. The musty smell of hotel air conditioning permeated his aqua blue polo shirt. The whole range of my vision was aqua—the signature color of The Gull Motel. Its roof had aqua trim, the windows were edged in the same paint, and the sign squatting on top of a twenty foot pole in the parking lot boasted a white seagull outlined against an aqua sky.

"Before lunch?" I questioned, the vacationer in me at war with my responsible side.

Uncle Mike opened the back hatch and manhandled my suitcase. He nodded toward his beloved motel. "You're a special occasion," he said. "Vacation is important. Trust me. I've built a business on it."

For the long drive from Michigan—where autumn had started to show its colors—I wore old comfortable knee-length shorts and a t-shirt, but I was overdressed now. The clientele here was more short-shorts and spaghetti straps than college dorm casual. I could adjust. This was not my first trip to the Gulf Coast.

I followed Uncle Mike through the office—dingy but familiar—and paused as he deposited my suitcase behind the desk. Rita, the receptionist, had a phone hooked between her ear and shoulder as she simultaneously checked in a guest. Somehow she managed to wave to me and give me a raised eyebrow smile. An experienced multi-tasker, Rita could probably smoke a cigarette, do her nails, and handle three guest complaints at the same time. She pointed toward the patio.

Movement—blurred by condensation—grabbed my attention. When my uncle slid the door open, a blonde tornado hit me. I'd been coming to The Gull several times a year all my life. One fact I could still count on was that Aunt Carol got smaller with age but her hair got bigger. Compensation comes in many forms.

She pulled me into a tight hug. "You need a nice cold drink."

Carol hauled me over to a concrete table surrounded by old metal chairs. The patio was large enough for several tables and chairs, all shaded by aqua umbrellas. The cracked concrete floor surrounded by a knee-high concrete wall didn't necessarily invite guests to linger, but the view did.

The wide white Florida beach ending in a sparkling blue Gulf of Mexico said *resort* even if the stacked two story building with parking right outside the rooms said *1950s beach motel.*

Carol raised the pitcher—also filled with aqua liquid continuing the theme of The Gull—and started to fill three glasses. She didn't get to the third before Rita shoved the glass door open and leaned out with the cordless phone.

"Better take this one, Carol," she said, holding out the phone.

Mike parked himself across from me while his wife went inside. "Your aunt's all excited to have you down here for a few weeks. I think she wants to pick your brain about making a few updates around here. Figures you got some great ideas with your degree."

Fresh from college and an internship to polish off my hotel and hospitality management degree, I wouldn't be bragging to say I had some ideas. But telling my aunt and uncle they'd have to spiff up The Gull for a new generation that didn't remember the moon landing was going to be a tough sell. They loved the old place just as it was. Truth is, so did I. I also loved my ancient slippers, but I wouldn't wear them on a date.

"I think she wants someone to go shopping with, too," he said, his broad smile highlighting deep wrinkles around his eyes and stretching out his age spots.

"I could shop," I agreed. "My college clothes won't work if I can land a spot in the management trainee program I applied to."

"The Grand Chicago. Heck of a fancy place," Uncle Mike said, raising his glass and clinking mine. "I'll drink to that."

Thinking about the gleaming floors, modern luxury, and five-star everything at the place where I hoped to start in January gave me a little feeling of disloyalty. I would always love The Gull. So what that it was a used Chevy and the Grand Chicago was a Rolls Royce? I'd put in a lot of miles in a Chevrolet.

Carol left the sliding door gaping behind her, striding quickly to our sunny table on the patio.

"My mother got arrested again," she said, picking up one of the margarita glasses and slamming half of it.

Mike pulled Carol onto his lap and shook his head sympathetically. "What was it this time?"

"Trespassing again. One of her card buddies bailed her out, but the police chief thinks she needs a babysitter. That was him on the phone."

"He's a nice enough guy. But we're starting to know him better than we should," Mike said. "Does this mean someone's headed for Michigan?"

Carol's mother, Aunt Gwen to me, was pushing eighty and still did water aerobics, played cards, and hosted wine-making classes at her lakeside cabin. Located next to a vineyard, the owners used to look the other way when Aunt Gwen gathered grapes near her property line for her little hobby. I'd heard she sent them a bottle every Christmas as a neighborly gesture. However, the vineyard changed hands a few years ago and the new owners see her actions as more theft than eccentricity.

"Maybe just for a week until we can talk some sense into her or build a big enough fence," Carol said.

"Too bad she refuses to move down here. Says Florida is for old people."

"Sounds like you'll need reinforcements this time." Uncle Mike blew out a long breath. "We haven't had a vacation in a long time, and Michigan's nice in the fall. Guess we'll figure out someone to watch over the place while we're gone."

They exchanged a glance and turned a laser-beam look on me, making me feel like the one guy who knew the combination in a bank that was being robbed. They glanced away quickly like a search light moving on to its next target.

The loyal niece in me wanted to say *sure, coach, send me in. I have a degree in hotel management, am nice to children and animals, and always flush the toilet.*

The vacationer in me wanted to say…uh…*I'm on vacation.*

Carol sucked both lips into her mouth and watched a seagull fly over. Mike scratched the short whiskers on his chin and toed a chip in the concrete.

I tried drinking for distraction and effect. Not that I could sustain that tactic for long. I can't hold my booze and I tend to crack under pressure faster than chapped lips in a Michigan winter.

"Maybe I could—"

Yelling and barking exploded next door and a half-naked man chased a huge yellow dog out of Harvey's Pirate Emporium and toward The Gull.

I jumped up. "Tulip!" Tulip was a three-year-old yellow Lab who did not know she wasn't a puppy anymore. She stole things, slept in inappropriate locations, ate stray cigarette butts, and was probably going to come home with a tattoo one of these days.

"Not again," Carol said.

Tulip skidded to a stop, dropped something shapeless and slobbery on the patio at my feet, and put her front paws on my shoulders. I sat down hard in my metal chair, off balance and getting licked like a tootsie pop. I was afraid she'd actually find out how many licks it took to get to my center.

The man sweating and breathing hard as he finished the race behind the dog already knew how many licks it took to get to my center. Skip McComber had circled me for years, a bonus temptation every time I visited my aunt and uncle's motel where he'd been the maintenance man since we were both sixteen. Last spring, the circle tightened considerably, aided by a reckless spring break attitude and fueled by tequila.

I stood up and tried to compose myself discretely. He looked as tempting as always. Tall, shirtless, eyes and hair the color of caramel splashed with sunshine. In contrast, I looked like a refugee from a pajama party. Shorts twisted, t-shirt violated, ponytail askew. Given the heat burning my cheeks, it was safe to assume I was flushed like an eighty-year-old jogger.

"This must be yours," I said, picking up the leather toolbelt Tulip had dropped at my feet. Covered in dog slime and punctured with teethmarks in several places, it was the dog's latest indiscretion. I could sympathize. Skip was my most recent fling, too.

He took the toolbelt and made a slow show of slinging it around his hips. He kept eye contact with me the whole time, like he was daring me to watch his seductive buckling up. I only let my eyes slide south once. I *was* on vacation. And he looked that good.

"Sorry about that," my aunt said. "Tulip thinks it's a chew toy. At least your tools are still in it this time and not scattered all over the sand. Most of them anyway."

He broke his focus on me and smiled at my aunt. "It's my fault for encouraging her to visit me." He dug a treat out of his pocket and flipped it to the dog. She caught it in midair and tossed him a look of slutty affection.

"Savvy just rolled in a few minutes ago," Carol said.

"I can see that," Skip said.

"She was supposed to be enjoying a vacation after all her hard work in college," Mike added, "but something has come up back home in Michigan with Carol's mother."

"Hope Aunt Gwen's okay," Skip said. "She's a hoot."

Carol rolled her eyes. "She's a crazy old lady. Arrested again for liberating grapes from the neighboring vineyard."

"Probably only stole what she was going to eat."

"Or make into wine," Mike said. "We were just talking to Savvy here about taking care of The Gull for us while we make a quick trip North."

Mike, Carol, Skip, and even Tulip stood in a line, looking at me like I had a stash of free tickets to Disney World. Except Tulip maybe. She probably hoped I had bacon in my pockets.

"I believe I was just about to say yes," I said with as much cheerful enthusiasm as possible. Of course I wanted to help my aunt and uncle. Hospitality is my business. And how hard could it be to manage a twenty-four room beach motel with an established clientele and a dedicated staff?

"Forgot to tell you we lost our maintenance man last month," Mike said, nodding at Skip. "He bought the bar next door and he's fixing it up."

"Harvey's Pirate Emporium?" I asked.

"Yep," Skip said. "But I got rid of Harvey already."

Harvey was a larger-than-life pirate statue who stood, shading his eyes like a tobacco store Indian,

14

outside the bar entrance. After a few drinks, he looked either friendlier or more sinister, depending on the drunk.

"Gave me the willies," Skip said, shrugging one shoulder. "Got him in cold storage in an old walk-in freezer."

"Won't be the same without him," I said. What I was really thinking was that The Gull wouldn't be the same without Skip and his extraordinary ability with his hands. "Who's our new maintenance man?"

"Don't have one. Muddling through for now, calling Skip over for emergencies," Uncle Mike said.

"I can change light bulbs, but I draw the line at using a plunger."

"That'll work," Carol said.

"Any other surprises I should know about?" I asked.

I thought a trace of tension transmitted from Carol to Mike to Skip, but Tulip didn't seem to notice and I thought I was just seeing mirages in the heat.

"Gotta go," Skip said. He ruffled Tulip's ears, flicked me a look, and strode across the ten yards of sand separating his bar from my—temporary—motel. I had extension cords longer than the space between our buildings, and it was going to be one tough job keeping my focus on The Gull while my aunt and uncle were away.

Chapter Two

"Got a new computer system since last time you were here," Rita announced. Rita is a thirty-something receptionist with the sun damage of a sixty-something sailor. She also has the colorful vocabulary of a sailor, but she usually keeps things PG when guests are within earshot. She'd been thrumming her colorful nails on the office counter for at least a decade and could probably teach me a lot about running The Gull.

"For reservations or other things?" I asked.

"Everything. Your aunt and uncle did a major upgrade a couple of months ago. Got the reservation system going and consolidated all kinds of documents and records."

"Maybe they're getting serious in their old age," I said.

Rita laughed. "Sure. Probably why Carol celebrates everything by getting out the margarita machine." She pointed to a cabinet below the Truman-era laminate countertop. "She keeps it right there, just in case you need to use it too."

"You better show me the new computer system first," I said.

She jiggled the mouse and the screen came to life, casting a colorful glow on Rita's tight white t-shirt, its deep v-neck leaving no doubt about the exposure of her cleavage to the sun.

Although we're both in the neighborhood of 5'7" and our natural hair color is light brown, the resemblance ends there. Her hair has blond streaks and chunks and is always teased to a certain height around her face. Mine is poker straight and has never seen a box of Miss Clairol. Rita had curves under her t-shirt and two-inch inseam shorts. My bookishly thin frame was concealed under a boxy t-shirt and baggy shorts.

"Think I can pull this off?" I asked. "Managing The Gull until they get back?"

She paged through several screens, focusing on the computer and avoiding eye contact. "Don't see why not. You're smart, you're family. Probably gonna inherit it someday anyway."

"No way."

"Why not? You're their only young relative. And what else would they do with it? I don't think they want it landing in the hands of some big company that doesn't care about it. Old places like this are getting snapped up all along the strip. Developers probably plan to knock down ugly old eyesores and put in chain hotels. The kind with continental breakfasts and rewards points."

"The Gull's not an eyesore," I protested.

"Just saying," Rita continued, "it's sitting on a nice chunk of beach. Skip must've mortgaged a fortune to get Harvey's Pirate Emporium before some developer did."

"Maybe," I mumbled, feeling streaks of warmth creep up my neck at the mention of my shirtless neighbor. I tried to refocus on the computer and get my mind in a cooler climate.

Rita stopped fiddling with the mouse and leaned on the counter, looking at me like she could read my secrets on my face.

I tried to evade her gaze by pretending to look very interested in the spreadsheet and tables on the screen. However, in addition to hiding behind my brains whenever possible, I also have the character attribute of being a bad liar. A complete novice at social deception—even when it would be a hell of a lot more convenient.

Rita possessed the people-reading gene, a skill very handy in a frontline receptionist at a motel with a colorful and varied clientele. She also dallied in gossip as a professional—or at least semipro—hobby.

"You've tangled with Skip," she said. It was not a question. It was a proclamation made in her experienced adult female voice.

"Not tangled," I said. "Not exactly. More like a long-term friendship."

"Right. He's been working here since he was sixteen and gets better looking every year. You've been coming here your whole life. I never quite believed you were just friends all that time. No surprise you got a little something going on with him. I would if I wasn't a little too *mature* for him."

She cocked her head and I knew I might as well open my diary and point out the page with the Skip episode. Figuratively speaking, of course. My one night stand with Skip still burned so deep that I would be afraid to immortalize it in pen, just in case it made it more impossible to somehow erase. Invisible ink wouldn't even help me under the scrutiny of Rita. She'd see through anything I made up now, especially since I was stalling. In my amateur liar status, I was out of my league with Rita.

"I wouldn't call it tangling," I muttered, sounding lame and junior high even to myself.

"Call it what you want, but I'm sure going to enjoy hearing that story one of these days."

"I'd prefer to forget about it," I said.

Rita rifled through a drawer for scrap paper and a pen. "Gonna be tough with him right next door using power tools and flaunting his tan."

"I'll try anyway."

Rita shoved the paper and pen toward me. "Might want to write some of this stuff down so you don't forget."

"About Skip?"

She shook her head, grinning at me like I was the only one wearing a tuxedo to a toga party. "About the computer. I'm supposed to be showing you how to run this system, but it's gonna be pretty hard if all you can think about is the boy next door."

****

The next night, I stood with the small staff of The Gull and watched my aunt and uncle get ready to roll out of The Gull's parking lot. Rita and I were flanked by the two full-time maids, Maria and LeeAnn. Skip came over for the occasion, too, as an emeritus employee and friend.

"We're so glad you're here to watch over the place," Carol whispered to me as she hugged me goodbye. "Barefoot Key isn't the place it used to be."

I wanted to ask what she meant, but she moved quickly to her long-time employees to dispense goodbye hugs.

"You take good care of our Gull, Savvy," Mike said. He motioned me over to the trunk of their car where he fiddled with arranging their luggage. In a low voice, he said, "I hope we're only gone a week at the most. I'd like to be back for the next Chamber of Commerce meeting. Businesses here in the Key are dropping like flies." He looked more serious than I'd ever seen him. "Now's the time we all gotta stick together."

"Don't worry about The Gull," I said lightly. "I'll only sell it off if I get enough cash to open the bait shop I've always dreamed of."

"I hope to bail the old gal out and be back before anyone notices we're gone," he said, shutting the trunk. He put one arm around my shoulders and gave me a quick squeeze. "And I won't worry knowing I have the smartest person in the family in charge down here."

They climbed in, we caught one last glimpse of big blond hair in the passenger side window, and Aunt Carol and Uncle Mike were gone. Tulip leaned against my leg, watching the departure along with us. She licked my ankle and gave me sad eyes.

"We need a drink," Maria said. "My mother-in-law's putting the kids to bed tonight because I figured it would be a late one."

LeeAnn looked at her watch.

"It's gonna be a late one, right?" Maria said. "I need a break from those kids."

Maria had four kids under the age of ten. Her husband drove a semi and only stayed home long enough to get his wife pregnant and his tires changed. The kids who weren't old enough for the joy of public education spent the day tailing their mother's housekeeping cart, torturing Tulip, or turning the swimming pool into a wave pool.

"Hell yeah," LeeAnn said. "I had a date with some fish tacos, but they'll wait."

"I found the owner's manual for the margarita machine and I think I can pull it off," I said. I thought this was a good time to show confidence in front of my staff.

"We could get started with the hooch while LeeAnn runs home and cooks for us," Skip offered.

"Bite me," LeeAnn said.

Divorced, thirty, and no kids, LeeAnn had a grouchy side that flirted with bitter. If there were honeymooners in the motel, she always got special assignment in some other area. Only one thing made her happy—cooking. And her fish tacos made other people happy, so it balanced out.

"Have they ever gone on vacation before?" I asked. My whole life, it had never occurred to me to wonder. Living in a beach motel in Florida seemed like a permanent vacation, but I wondered for the first time if they'd ever actually gone away. They didn't come to my college graduation because they had a full house and a fishing tournament in town. I told them they weren't missing anything because college ceremonies were notoriously dull.

"Not that I know of," Rita said. "Carol's gone home a few times. They've been on a few overnighters or weekenders I can think of. But leaving for a week, both of them? Can't remember a time. Guess they figure they can do it this time because you're here."

"They trust all of you," I said. "You're like family."

"But you *are* family," LeeAnn said. "They know you won't lock the doors and have an orgy."

Everyone turned and stared at LeeAnn.

"Not that we would," she said.

Their taillights were long gone down the access road The Gull shared with the Sunshine Souvenir Stand on one side and Skip's bar on the other side. Not technically a street, the two lanes of blacktop leading to our three businesses were owned by the Sunshine and ran across a chunk of its property.

Although my aunt and uncle were out of sight, I still stared in the direction they'd gone, feeling like a little girl entrusted with playing house for real. How bad could I screw up? They'd be home before I even had to order more toilet paper. And maybe this would be a good opportunity for me to bolster my resume and improve my chance of getting into the trainee program. The experience columns on my application were emptier than a beach with a shark sighting. Probably the reason for my wait-list status on the program.

"I've got a good feeling about their trip," Maria said. "They'll get the old bat straightened out and have fun seeing the trees turning colors up north. We should drink to them."

"A feeling, huh?" LeeAnn asked.

Maria nodded seriously. LeeAnn sighed like a sibling who was tired of her little sister. Although not remotely related, the two housekeepers had been a team for at least a decade. I used to call them Miss Maria and Miss LeeAnn until they told me to knock it off sometime during my first year of college.

"Got some stuff in the cooler next door," Skip offered. "Be right back."

We all checked out his ass as he swung across the parking lot.

"That's one fine package," LeeAnn said.

"Shit," Rita said, grinning.

"We could share him," Maria said. "He likes kids and tacos."

Rita glanced over at me but didn't say anything. Whatever she suspected about my relationship with Skip, she was keeping it under her highlights for now.

"I bet he likes tacos more," LeeAnn said.

"All men do," Rita said.

Chapter Three

The shed full of pool equipment might as well have been part of the launch pad for the space shuttle. I faced a large cylinder, a whole series of pipes and hoses, and several sealed containers with hazardous materials labels on them.

I wrinkled my nose at the clean chemical chlorine smell, crossed my arms over my chest, and faced the giant pool pump. It probably smelled better than I did in my sweaty t-shirt, shorts, ancient sneakers, and sticky ponytail. It was hot in the shed, the afternoon sun abusing its metal roof. Still, I wanted to appear brave, not flinching in the face of a whole room full of equipment I couldn't tell from a garbage disposal.

Day four of what I had planned as a Gulf Coast vacation had me perspiring in the pool shed and wondering what I should do.

"Need any help?"

I whipped around, blood rushing from surprise and something else. Of course I knew the voice. Skip McComber leaned against the frame of the open shed door. Shirtless. Wearing low slung jeans and a grin that registered somewhere between caution and amusement.

He looked like a man who knew how to run a pool pump. From experience, I knew he could handle a lot more than that.

"I'm fine," I said, trying for cheerful dismissal in my tone. "Just taking a look around."

"Taking stock of your new property."

"Temporary property."

"Since it's your place now and all," he said, disregarding my comment, "looks like we'll be seeing a lot of each other."

A mild earthquake rolled under my sternum and sent shockwaves from its epicenter. Maybe I'd have better luck with the space shuttle launch pad configuration than I would handling Skip.

"Temporary," I repeated.

He nodded, continuing to appraise me with his look. Perhaps appraisal was too glamorous a word. He was looking at me like a cat who'd just opened the bird cage and was wondering how much fun he could have with the bird.

Skip had been rattling my cage since we were both sixteen. Every time I came to visit my aunt and uncle for a vacation, an added perk had been the endorphin boost from their local boy turned maintenance man. A skinny handsome kid, he had matured every time I came back to the Gull until he was the full-blown man standing in front of me.

"I know a lot about fixing things," he said.

Of course he did. He had the benefit of owning a penis, a wonderful device imparting knowledge about cars, computers, pool pumps, and probably the space shuttle. I also was acquainted first hand with Skip's expertise in using his member—a fact reminding me why I had to get out of the overheated shed.

"I'll keep that in mind just in case," I said. "I have to go check on the…um…air conditioning units."

He smiled, not giving up his post blocking the exit. "Planning to recharge the condensers?"

I know a challenge when I see one. I also know enough not to swing around a sword with my eyes closed. Recharge a condenser? If Skip thought he was going to exact some masculine advantage over me by testing my mechanical knowledge, he had a surprise coming.

He was going to discover how humiliatingly easy that would be.

But I hadn't gutted my way through college to be vanquished by an air conditioner or a pool pump. Or the sexy male renovating the bar next door. He'd have to go push buttons on his power equipment because my buttons were off limits.

"There are plenty of things that I should consider recharging around here," I said, side stepping through the doorway and taking care not to touch any part of Skip's delicious body. He did not make that easy for me. Somehow, his scent—man soap mixed with sawdust—erased the chlorine smell and took me back to spring break before I could put on the brakes.

"I hope I'm one of them," he said, filling the doorway with his broad shoulders.

"Not on the books," I said. "Got plenty of other things that need attention."

It's true that I was shutting him down before he even got going, but it was the only way. I couldn't be rational in my relationship with Skip. After last spring's foolish step into the land beyond friendship, I didn't have the credentials in the romance department to handle a casual relationship. He had to stay next door or I would lose my grip on myself and The Gull.

"Savvy," he said, his tone stopping me. I turned to face him, not wanting to be rude, not knowing what to do about him next door, not knowing if air conditioners even had condensers.

"Come over sometime. I'll buy you a beer."

"Not a huge offer from a man who owns a bar," I said.

He grinned. "Doesn't mean it's not a good offer."

"I'm not on spring break," I said. *And that was six months ago.* We'd exchanged cell phone numbers at dawn and never used them once. "And I have to get to work."

"Have to check the circuit boards on the shower heads?" he asked, the corners of his mouth inching up.

"Don't be ridiculous," I said. Of course I know shower heads and electronics don't mix. Maybe some fancy ones in the fancy catalogs, but I knew we didn't have anything like that around The Gull. At least, I was pretty sure. And I was already getting tired of his mechanical superiority. I'm savvy about a lot of things he probably doesn't know the first thing about.

"I'm working on a business plan for The Gull while I'm managing it. Projecting ROI. Spreadsheets. Metrics. Stuff like that."

Skip studied me for a moment, making me believe I had the upper hand.

"Hard to imagine what your return on investment is gonna be when you haven't had to sink anything in an investment," he said. "You want to talk ROI sometime, I'll show you the pile of debts I've racked up renovating the Pirate Emporium."

I'd been inside the Pirate Emporium plenty of times, none of which would have inspired me to pay much for the place or sink any gold doubloons into it. On the scale of tackiness, it was a few notches lower than The Gull. Or at least in the same neighborhood.

"Maybe sinking a bunch of money in a renovation isn't your best choice," I said, feeling a hitch in my craw. I should be directing guests to the concierge desk in a five-star hotel, not discussing metrics in shorts and flip-flops. Especially not with a shirtless man who made me wish we were both naked.

"Think I should leave it in its tacky 1950s Florida condition?"

I shrugged, trying to appear cool and remember what we were talking about. "Lots of people like that." I gestured at The Gull. "This place seems to be doing fine."

"You're in for some surprises if you think things are fine here in Barefoot Key," he said, his tone suggesting—again—that he knew something I didn't. Maybe it was his penis. He couldn't help himself. But I still didn't have to play his game.

"Why are you here?" I asked. I wanted him to go away before I sweated through my t-shirt.

"Just saying hello."

"And?"

Skip blew out a breath and hitched his tool belt a little higher. The muscles in his chest and arms rippled with the movement.

"Maybe I just wanted to see—" his words trailed off as he looked over the pool deck and the back patio.

Tulip was dutifully prowling the perimeter of the deck, the sunshine reflecting off her yellow fur. She edged closer to the inviting blue pool, her long tongue reaching down to lap some water. The dog looked around and I knew what she was going to do a split second before it happened.

Tulip jumped in, happily dog paddling in the cool water. The lone guest in the pool, a young boy supervised by his mom lounging in a chair, laughed and tossed Tulip the ball he was playing with. His mother looked up from her novel and shaded her eyes, watching the giant wet animal circling her son and nosing the ball through the water.

"Tulip," I yelled, jumping over a low hedge. The dog was in heaven, intoxicated by the midday cooldown. She ignored me like a penguin ignores ice.

"Tulip! Get out!" I pointed to the pool deck and gave her the official *you're in big trouble* look.

Right behind me, I felt Skip's presence. It wasn't just the Florida sun. There were actual heat waves emanating from his bare chest—tanned with a light covering of caramel colored hair—and whisking over me.

I turned and caught his look. He was laughing, the clean muscles of his abdomen contracting with the effort.

"Tulip," I scolded. "Get out now." I gestured authoritatively again, but the usually obedient dog was wrapped up in the siren song of the water.

Skip picked the pool net off its hook on the back fence, scooped up the ball, and flipped it onto the sand. Tulip heaved herself over the side of the pool, leaving a river of water on the deck. She didn't even take time to shake off before she barreled after the ball and caught it in her teeth, rolling in the sand until she was completely caked, a living sand sculpture.

"Thank you," I said sarcastically to Skip, "That was very helpful."

He shrugged. "Got her out before those bastards from the health department found out about it."

"Much appreciated."

Skip tapped his head and smiled at me. "I can be savvy, too," he said. He turned and sauntered across the deck, forcing me to share the view of his backside with the lounging mom by the pool. She abandoned her book completely and feasted her eyes on the man candy heading next door.

"I hope she follows you home," I shouted after him, consoling myself by imagining Tulip shaking a maelstrom of sand and water all over my hot but troublesome neighbor's bar.

****

Several nights later, I was holed up in room twenty-four. Ever since high school when my parents decided I was old enough for my own room, my aunt and uncle had been reserving this room for me. It was at the top of the open staircase on the far end of the motel. As an end room, it had a window overlooking the bar next door. The interior had not changed in decades—an aqua bedspread and curtains with a tile floor and a no-frills bathroom. I'd changed a lot in the last decade, celebrating graduations from high school and college with many vacations and spring breaks in between. And last spring, I'd shared the bed in this room for the first time.

The only nod to modernization room twenty-four could boast was a newish flatscreen TV over the dresser. It was small, but I only needed enough screen to view my favorite nightly quiz show. I pulled shredded cheese from the mini-fridge, dumped it on a plate of nachos, and popped it into the motel-sized microwave. With a cold beer for good measure, I'd just settled in for my guilty pleasure when someone knocked on my door. I ignored it, wanting some solitude and a chance to feel smart. It was my way to recharge. And I needed it. Aunt Carol and Uncle Mike's emails indicated I might be in for a long tenure as The Gull's guardian.

Tonight's game show categories were just being revealed when the knocking went into round two. Louder. I slapped to the door in bare feet and pulled aside the aqua curtains to peek out. Big mistake. There was no pretending I wasn't in my room when more than six feet of man lounged against my door and watched me through the window. As the motel's former and sometimes maintenance man, he probably still had a key to my room anyway.

One shoulder on the door, eyes on me, Skip was a walking temptation. I opened the door.

"Just stopped by to see if you could use any help," Skip said.

With the game show, no. I know all those answers. With running the Gull? Maybe. But I wasn't admitting that.

I composed my expression into front desk neutral. "Everything's under control," I said.

"Everything?"

"Unless smoke's rolling from one of the rooms and there's a naked dog in the pool. Then yes. Under control."

Skip nodded. "Guess I should have figured."

I thought he might turn on his workbooted heel and walk the open hallway down to the aqua-railed concrete stairs. But he didn't. I heard laughter and applause from the television behind me. The TV host was probably being witty and charming, making guests on the show feel at home and smart. And I was missing it. Right then, I didn't feel at home or particularly smart.

"How long have they been gone?" he asked. He didn't have to say who he meant.

"A week."

"And?"

"And they're not sure how much longer. Aunt Gwen's slipped the groove a little. They're looking into a babysitter to keep her out of trouble."

"So you're gonna keep on holding down the fort while they're gone?"

I crossed my arms over my chest, wishing I had my glasses to look over at him. "As a matter of fact, I plan to convert the lobby into a pirate-themed bar. Drive the guy next door out of business."

Skip laughed. "Hell, I'm not even in business yet. Hoping to open end of October, but there's a lot to get done in the next six weeks if that's going to happen."

"Then I'm sure you're very busy," I said in what I hoped was a dismissive tone.

He reached out and laid two fingers right below my neck in the little notch where my collar bones meet. He leaned close, the two fingers the only actual contact between us but suggesting a whole lot more. I knew he could feel my heart thumping with those two fingers.

"Remember that spring I started working here? You came down for spring break and I took you out for ice cream?" he said.

"We drove down the coast for almost two hours. I thought you were kidnapping me."

He smiled. "I couldn't resist. I had a new license and a used Jeep."

"As I recall, that Jeep was three different colors."

"Plus primer."

"Four colors," I said. I vividly remembered that day. Spring sun, freedom, and a guy who sent my high school hormones through the roof. I was torn between running away with him and insisting he drive me home before my aunt and uncle called the state police. We pulled off and watched the ocean and he told me about his father's fishing charter. I'd told him about my dreams of running an elegant hotel.

We got ice cream, and we got home before the sun set. I remember thinking how strange it was that my aunt and uncle hadn't said a word. My parents had been a lot pickier about dating, so much so that I felt like I was getting away with something even to go to the movies. Life was freer in Barefoot Key. Then, but not now.

"Too bad we're not sixteen anymore," I said.

"We could pretend."

I shook my head. "I don't have the freedom to run away for the day. I have to manage this place. People are counting on me."

Skip looked like he was going to argue, but he dropped his hand and broke the connection between us.

"Call me if you need help with the final game show question." He spun and swaggered down the outside corridor and disappeared down the steps toward the beach.

I shut the door firmly and slid the bolt in place. Barring a fire or a hurricane, I would not be opening that door again tonight. Settling in with a beer and a plate of cold chips halfway through the final round, I tried to focus on what I knew.

"This Florida College began as a school for the deaf and now houses freshmen in the historic Ponce De Leon hotel on its campus," the quiz show host said.

Just as the answer rolled to the tip of my tongue, my cell phone chirped.

"Flagler College," the text read.

Skip McComber is under the false impression that he can run my pool pump, manage my dog, tell me quiz show answers, and get under my skin.

Chapter Four

Uncle Mike had long held a seat and the job of community relations coordinator for the Barefoot Key Chamber of Commerce. When asked, he couldn't tell me exactly what the job entailed, but he said I'd figure it out. One more example of people giving me credit for being more savvy than I really am.

The Chamber of Commerce met in the birthday party room at the putt-putt golf course near the pier downtown. Only a few frazzled parents were chasing colored balls around with short clubs while their children alternately cheated or complained in the waning Florida sun. So we had the place mostly to ourselves, with only a bored teenager working the front window and handing out little pencils and scorecards.

The fifteen members of the Chamber who were present represented a wide variety of tourist attractions and other businesses in Barefoot Key, some existing for decades. In its heyday, the town had a population of nearly fifteen thousand permanent residents. A tourist boom in the 1950s upped that number exponentially and left its mark wherever you looked. Many small motels and shops like The Gull and the Sunshine Souvenir Stand were still doing business. But there were abandoned motels, roadside stands, and diners on the fringes of town. Years ago, Barefoot Key was a perfect stopover for the night as tourists drove down the Gulf Coast in search of Florida adventures and sunshine. But times had changed.

These days, people moved faster, preferring the highway as they hustled toward big cities and theme parks. I wondered if people were ready to go back to a different time when it was about the Gulf Coast journey, not the roller-coaster destination. Maybe I was old-fashioned. Certainly I was nostalgic about the place I'd vacationed dozens of times.

"Randy Fischer," a man said, vigorously shaking my hand and pulling me out of my folding chair so everyone could see me. "I own a golf cart rental downtown. Look me up if you ever need one."

He put a hand on my shoulder and turned me to face the members present. "Like you to meet Savvy

Thorpe. Mike's niece. She'll be running The Gull until Mike and Carol get back from taking care of Carol's mother in Michigan."

"Not an easy job," a woman said. I wondered if she meant running The Gull or running after Aunt Gwen. She wore a black apron with an embroidered ice cream cone on the front and plenty of remnants of ice cream servings. Her short white hair contrasted with the hot pink reading glasses on top of her head. "Sally Broomfeld," she said, leaning across the table and shaking my hand. "I own Sally's Scoops, two locations in town."

"How long have Carol and Mike been gone?" Randy asked.

"Almost two weeks."

"Heard from 'em?" Sally asked.

I nodded. "Today. Aunt Carol said her mother's not being her usual difficult self."

"Is that good or bad?" Sally asked.

"Not sure. They think maybe she has dementia and it's not just a simple matter of bailing her out and paying her court costs anymore."

"So they'll be gone longer," Sally said. "I'm curious about what you want to do with The Gull. Any big plans while they're gone?"

"I'm not authorized to do much new. I'm a placeholder more than an actual manager."

"You're related aren't you?" Randy asked. "Relatives don't need permission. Especially since they're probably not paying you much."

They were paying me enough to make the first installment on my student loan. Combined with free room and board, I actually had forty-two bucks in my purse. If it went on much longer, I'd have to start using the full kitchen in my aunt and uncle's owner's suite, but I was getting by on take-out, frozen food, and ambition for now.

Randy introduced the other members, most of them names and business I recognized from many trips to Barefoot Key over the years and from hearing my aunt and uncle talk about their friends and neighbors. Skip's father, Jude McComber, relaxed in an ocean blue McComber's Charters t-shirt at the end of the table. He looked like an older and more sun-exposed version of Skip. Except he was wearing a shirt.

The meeting came to order. A reading of the minutes from the last meeting was waived and the "new business" part of the program was a hushed and tense discussion about some local businesses that were recently sold. Their owners, although members of the Chamber, were not present.

"Wonder who's gonna be next?" Jude McComber asked.

The already serious mood of the meeting dipped into funeral-mood.

"Come on," Sally said. "We should talk about something fun. Like the annual event."

From the conversation that followed, I learned about the annual fall fundraiser to promote local businesses and fund chamber expenses and advertising for the rest of the year. After listening for about ten minutes, I realized no one had any good ideas for a themed event and the date was only a month away. There had been half-hearted suggestions of a casino night or a wine and cheese party. Someone had even ponied up

Karaoke as a potential idea. After decades of doing the annual fundraiser, it appeared they were tapped out.

I couldn't take the floundering much longer. "How about an Old Florida theme?" I suggested.

Eyes cut in my direction. "How do you mean?" someone asked.

"We could capitalize on our location, really sell the town's history going back decades as a tourist stopover. Offer t-shirts and souvenirs with orange blossoms and palm trees. Stuff like that," I concluded, not convinced anyone was buying what I was trying to sell.

"Sounds like a typical day around here," Randy said. "We need to try something fresh, something modern tourists want that'll drive 'em here and not places that got hotels with pools on the roof and fountains as big as Niagara Falls."

"Isn't it possible that people are tired of those places? Maybe they want nostalgia," I argued. "Roadside fruit stands. Water-skiing shows."

People exchanged glances, shook their heads, and muttered a little. I knew these were tough times for local businesses. I'd seen the empty properties dotting the streets like a polka dot pattern, practically every other building in some locations as if a giant was using a checkerboard to pick off parcels of land.

Conversation about reviving the Old Florida mystique was officially stalled out now. My idea was a flat tire on their mopeds and my semi-professional blouse was retaining heat like plastic wrap. I'd agonized over wearing the shirt and now it felt like a medieval torture device. Rita had the right idea. Tank tops are the secret weapon against Gulf Coast heat.

Not that they'd help me sell this idea.

Randy Fischer turned toward me with a neutral expression. "I don't know about this. I'd think if 'old' was a selling point, we'd be doing a lot more selling around here. But I'm willing to listen. How long would you need to come up with some ideas?" he asked. "We could table this and come back in a week. But we really gotta get going."

One week to come up with a plan for an event I'd never attended in a town I only temporarily lived in. Since a year wouldn't be enough time, I didn't see the harm in agreeing to a week. It was like ripping off a band-aid. Better to do it fast and minimize the suffering.

"I can try," I said.

****

I sat on the laundry folding table, swinging my legs and hoping for momentum. Maria and LeeAnn loaded their housekeeping carts with fresh sheets, towels, soaps, and miniature hair products. While Maria had dark skin, eyes, and short, practical hair, LeeAnn was her opposite. Blond and brunette streaks colored her teased-on-top hair. LeeAnn was also a whole lot bustier than her friend and co-worker.

"Want to flip for top floor?" LeeAnn asked.

Maria cut her eyes to me. I overheard Rita telling her she better take the upper floor for the next few days because that's where a twenty-something honeymooning couple were staying in one room and a fifteenth-anniversary couple were in another. I'd run into both couples last evening and they looked too happy to risk LeeAnn.

"I'll do it," Maria said.

"Are you sure?"

"Uh-huh. I don't have kids in the pool or hanging off my cart today, so I don't mind."

"I need some fresh ideas," I said. "Something new."

Both maids swung their eyes to me. "Not much to change," LeeAnn said. "Rita gives us the check in and out list. We clean the rooms according to the list. We like to think they're nice and fresh."

"You know what I mean."

"Yep. But we're not the idea people," Maria said. "We're just the maids."

"Baloney. You could probably run this place better than I can."

"We could trade," LeeAnn said. "You clean the johns and I'll stand around in the office and watch Rita take reservations and run credit cards."

"Is that what my aunt and uncle did all day?"

"Not exactly. They were also the fire department, running around putting out little fires," Maria said.

"Most of those stupid little fires would have burned themselves out eventually anyway," LeeAnn commented. "People have too much drama."

"What you need is an aqua colored shirt. Maybe get the hotel logo embroidered on it. It'll get you in the spirit," Maria said.

I sighed, slumping on my temporary seat. "I hate aqua."

"Shit. Everybody born after 1979 hates aqua. Maybe we need a change," LeeAnn said. "It could be your first big rebellious move. They left you in charge."

"But told me not to change anything."

"Huh," LeeAnn huffed out. "That's bullshit. They don't really expect you to just keep the lights on and toilet paper on the rolls. I think they're just testing you out."

Maria shoved her cart toward the door and parked herself in a plastic chair older than I am. "Maybe you should tell us what your plans are. Assuming you've got some."

I rolled my shoulders and itched an imaginary spot on both elbows. Tulip wandered in and I scratched her ears while I put my thoughts into words. She brought in the smell of salt water and sand, reminding me what I loved about this place.

"I want to return it to them in better shape than I got it."

"But the same," LeeAnn said sarcastically.

"Yes."

"Not sure what they taught you in college, but that sounds like a dumbass idea."

"I need to gain some real experience as a manager so I can shore up my application to be in that manager trainee program at the Grand Chicago."

"You still hoping for that?" LeeAnn asked.

"Of course. That's what I went to school for, and I don't have any other prospects. I have student loans that aren't going to wash out with the tide."

"So you need to show your stuff," Maria said sympathetically.

I nodded. "And since I can't change things, I have to add things," I said.

Total silence for fifteen seconds.

"Right?" I asked.

"What are you gonna add?" Maria asked. "We have twenty-four rooms. That's that."

"I don't know. Perks, I guess."

LeeAnn laughed. "You're a cute girl, probably even pretty if you'd show some skin. But come on, what kind of perks are you thinkin' about?"

I rolled my eyes and slid off the table. "I'm going to take a walk on the beach before it gets hot and figure it out."

It was barely past eight o'clock in the morning, so I didn't have my Florida heat armor on. No sunscreen, no ponytail. I was also missing my academic armor. No glasses. Sunrise on the Gulf Coast is less impressive than sunset for obvious geographical reasons, but morning on any beach is beautiful. Some mysterious army of tractors pulling trailers rigged with giant rakes had already been by and combed the beach. I never thought about where that beach crew came from, but figured it was one of the city-funded perks of Barefoot Key.

I rolled my toes in and out of the grooves left in the sand, trying to get my thoughts in a groove. What kind of amenities could I offer guests that would fill rooms on quiet weekdays in the fall? What services could I tack on some extra fees for that people would jump at?

What did Barefoot Key and The Gull have as playing cards?

My parents were seasoned travelers. I could ask them for suggestions since they'd stayed in fifteen different hotels in all fifty states. But I needed to figure this out for myself.

I watched a fishing charter leave a wharf several properties farther down the beach. I could see at least half a dozen people and lots of long fishing poles sticking up all over the boat like a case of bed hair. An idea swirled through my head like the sand between my toes.

"Fishing charter," a voice said behind me.

I jumped. "You shouldn't sneak up on people like that."

"Hard to make noise in sand," Skip said.

"You should try. I might have had a heart attack or something and then you'd have my blood on your hands."

Skip picked up a long lock of hair brushing my shoulder and twisted it in his fingers. He leaned forward just a little and glanced down my shirt. "You look perfectly healthy to me."

I stepped back, hoping to restore my heart rate to something close to healthy.

"One of these days we should talk about last spring," he said. "Maybe over some tequila."

I narrowed my eyes at him. "I thought you would have called me if you wanted to talk. You've had plenty of time since April."

Skip put his hands in the pockets of his cargo shorts and rocked back on bare heels in the sand. He was shirtless as usual. And he wasn't taking my bait.

"Saw you staring at the fishing charter boat," he said.

"I was thinking about something."

"Thinking of teaming up with a local charter and offering package deals? Could be a great add-on to rooms at The Gull."

My heart rate steam-trained up the scale again. That was exactly the idea I'd been formulating, and I didn't appreciate him acting like it was his. Just like the Jeopardy incident the other night. The danger of years of slightly-lusty friendship is that you can know a person too well. And they've got your thoughts on speed-dial.

"I knew that answer," I said.

Skip tipped up one side of his face, giving me a questioning look.

"On Jeopardy. Flagler College. I knew that."

"Figured you did."

"So why did you text me the answer?"

"Maybe I wanted you to know I knew."

It was on the tip of my tongue to ask him why he cared what I thought about his brainpower, especially after six months of silence from him after our spring break fling that apparently ended almost six years of friendship. Or flirtation. Or both.

I decided to live to fight another day on that count.

"So how would that work? If I did offer a package?" I asked.

"You would make a deal with a local charter—"

"Know of any?"

Skip smiled. "I could talk to my dad about it if you want."

"And?"

"And you make it easy for guests to sign up, have them pay you in advance, keep a cut for yourself and share the rest with the charter company. Win-win."

"What's it in for the charter company?"

"Might help fill up some slow weekdays."

I thought about that for a few seconds. I was trying to fill up my slow weekdays, too.

"Might help you out with those slow days, too."

I let out a long slow breath. Either Skip could read minds or my thoughts were obvious as hell. I'd prefer to think of myself as a woman with a little mystery, but I guess I'll have to stick with cerebral instead of secretive.

"I'll think about it. If you happen to talk to your dad, you might ask him what he thinks."

"I can tell you already he'll say yes."

"What about you?"

"What about me?"

"Why aren't you working the family boat? I figured you'd be training to take over the business one of these days."

Skip dug a hole in the sand with his bare toes. "Don't know about that. Tourism isn't exactly booming on this part of the coast. Not room enough for both of us on that boat."

"So a bar instead?"

"Everybody drinks."

"But not everybody fishes."

"Think there's a proverb goes something like that," Skip said.

Seagulls swept down to the sand nearby, talking to other seagulls and sending their cries over the salty waves. Toes in the sand, early morning sun and breeze stirring my hair and brushing my skin, a half naked man within reach—it felt like vacation. Except it wasn't.

"Don't see why you have to do anything at all," Skip said.

"I have to run The Gull."

"I know. I mean I don't see why you have to do extra stuff." He tipped his head toward the motel across the beach. "It seems to be going along just fine as it is. Has for years."

"And I have to keep it that way until my aunt and uncle get back. If I return it in even better condition—"

Yelling from the Gull interrupted me. It was Rita. Standing on the pool deck, shading her eyes, and calling my name. Tulip stood next to her, barking to be helpful.

"Come in here," Rita yelled when she knew she had my attention. "And bring Skip with you."

He raised both eyebrows. "Breakfast invite, you think?"

"Don't think so."

"Mechanical problem?"

"Maybe."

"What were you saying about returning The Gull better than you got it?" he asked.

He might have been joking, but I didn't feel like explaining to Skip or anyone else how desperate I was to prove I could be successful in more than just a classroom. They could all think whatever they wanted as they watched me work up a sweat to improve the Gull's bottom line. I needed this to work, and it only took one glance at my student loan debt to understand why.

"You coming?" Rita yelled. Rita was tough, loyal, predictable, and a colorful dresser. But she didn't do subtle.

61

"Better go," I said. I turned and took a few steps, listening for Skip but hearing nothing but ocean. I glanced back. He hadn't moved.

"Are you coming with me?"

"Waiting to be asked. I don't work there anymore."

I faced him, hands on hips. "Fine. Will you please come into the motel with me?"

"Best offer I've had in..."

"Six months?"

"Didn't think we were going there, but yeah."

I shook my head, speechless but unable to stifle the start of a smile. This time when I headed for the motel, I heard soft swishing behind me.

Rita met us on the edge of the concrete patio. "Got a teenage drama queen stuck in the bathroom in room seventeen."

"Bad hair day?" I asked.

"Sticky door in seventeen. I swear I got that fixed for good last time," Skip said.

"Changes with the humidity. And the attitude of the person slamming it. In this case, we got a fifteen year old with her period and a momma she's sick of listening to."

"Deadly combination," I said.

"I'll see what I can do, but I'm not going in alone," Skip said. "And she better be wearing clothes."

I followed him to the stairs, Rita falling in right beside me. "Really ought to look into getting a full-time maintenance man," she said in a fake whisper they could hear as far as Tampa, "since our old one quit to open his own bar."

Skip stopped, one foot on the first stair riser. "Which is where all my tools are." He turned and brushed past us. "Hate to look like an amateur. Be right back."

We heard yelling and pounding from the open door on the second floor. "Think he's coming back?" Rita asked.

I listened to the shrill voices above our heads. Loud ones from an exasperated mother, muffled teenage sounds that sounded sulky even through a bathroom door.

"Would you?" I asked.

"Better tail him and drag him back. Make him a good offer for his services."

I rolled my eyes and trudged after Skip reasoning that it was more fun than going upstairs to the mother-daughter meltdown.

Chapter Five

"You sure this is a good idea?" Rita asked, eyeing the dozen or so women who'd checked into a block of rooms on the first floor.

"It'll be fun. They'll be fine." They were the first group of women signed up for my "Girl's Night Out" package. And they were loud and excited.

It seemed like a great idea. Team up with a local limo company, idle on a weeknight. Work with a local spa having a weekday in September slowdown. Take a group of gals for the works then a night out in downtown Barefoot Key. Limo them back to the motel to sleep it off. Rooms three through nine booked. No questions asked.

Women ranging in age from twenty five to fifty, hair color from pure to processed, and poundage from one hundred twenty and up hauled roller bags into the reception area of the office. They filled it with perfume and chatter until Rita cut me a glare and passed me a note.

"I need a Girl's Night Out for myself. Right now," the note said.

I shook my head. "No way. I need you to ride herd on this. You're tougher than any of them."

She looked unconvinced.

"And I have extra coupons for free manicures."

"Now you're talking," Rita said.

"Any chance of a late checkout?" a woman wearing a pink leopard-print shirt and fifty extra pounds asked.

"Usually an extra charge, but since you're here with the package deal, I think we can make that happen," Rita told her.

Rita and I both knew the rooms weren't booked until the following weekend anyway. That's why my package plan to fill up lonely weeknights at The Gull seemed especially justified now. I felt righteous in my business savvy and pulled off a genuine smile. I just hoped my other ideas were as successful as this.

The limo pulled up out front and a driver, black polyester suit and hat, appeared in the doorway. He looked overdressed in the shabby lobby but nonplussed by the perfume and noise. I figured limo drivers have seen it all. Twice. But they're probably sworn to secrecy.

"Give them ten minutes to get their luggage in their rooms, and then they'll be ready to hit the spa," I said, swiping my hair off my neck. All that female flesh overheated the small check-in area. Maybe I needed a full time air conditioning and maintenance man if I planned to do this very often. For the motel, I mean. I wondered if Skip would be willing to come back on a part-time arrangement. Maybe if I made him a good enough offer. I knew he was swimming in debt and I was not above capitalizing on that.

"Excuse me." The voice was right behind me, male, and unfamiliar.

A man wearing a yellow polo shirt and the kind of pants everyone knew came with a concealed elastic waist stood behind me with a clipboard. Age wise, he was somewhere between forty and eighty. Hard to tell.

"Are you with the limo company?" I asked.

"No."

I gestured toward the group of women. "Husband?"

He laughed and pushed his glasses higher on his nose. "Nope."

"Spa Company?"

He shook his head. "Florida Retired Traveler's Agency."

All the air left my body in a rush leaving me feeling like an angel food cake that had gone terribly wrong and ended up one inch tall in the bottom of the pan.

"I wasn't expecting you," I said, trying to sound professional and friendly despite the chaos of estrogen everywhere around us.

"I sent you a postcard asking if you'd be willing to do an interview for our magazine. You checked yes," the man said.

"I remember now." I shot Rita a look that telegraphed the word *emergency.* She returned a look that said *whatever he wants, good luck.* "I'm just surprised you were so prompt." I stuck out my hand. "I'm Savvy Thorpe. Manager of the motel while its owners are on an extended vacation."

His hand was a little sweaty—or maybe it was mine—but his handshake was firmer than the rest of him looked. "Dalton Longfellow."

"Nice to meet you. Would you mind sitting on the patio for a few minutes while I get this group to their destination?"

He looked dubiously at the all-female luggage brigade rolling in a wave toward the first floor rooms. "Bridal party?" he asked.

"Something like that," I said.

I slid the glass door open and pointed to a patio table, shaded from the late afternoon sun by an aqua umbrella. Longfellow parked himself in a chair and I muscled the door shut. The last of the spa group was wheeling out the side door that led to the parking side of the first floor.

All rooms on the bottom floor were two-doored. One entrance direct from the parking lot with a utilitarian door, one sliding door opening onto the beach on the other side. Second floor rooms only had one beachside door on the exterior hallway. I preferred the second floor for that reason. Having only one door cuts down on surprises.

"Shit," I whispered to Rita. "That guy is from the Florida Retired Traveler's Agency."

"Never heard of it," she said.

"The FRTA," I said, thinking the official initials would impress Rita.

Rita grinned. "The FRTA, huh? Rearrange it a little and you've got FART. They should call themselves the old fart agency."

I cut a look to the patio, but the door was firmly shut and no way could Longfellow hear us. "Those old farts have money to burn at motels," I said. "A good review from the magazine could really help us."

"Maybe if we want to fill the first floor," Rita said. "Always get dinged because we don't have an elevator and old people seem to think it's a necessity."

"Have we ever considered adding one?"

She shook her head. "Too expensive. Not worth the payoff."

"We've got plenty of other amenities to offer."

Rita raised both eyebrows. "Like what?"

"Good rates."

"Uh-huh."

"Clean rooms."

"Yeah."

Rita examined her nails, probably considering the free manicures I'd offered while she waited for me to work on my sales pitch.

"Great service," I said.

Rita scrunched her lips and shook her head very slowly side to side. "That all you got for polyester pants man out there?"

"Help me out."

"Tell you what. We have to use what we've got. We're old Florida at its best. Got the beachside location, not much traffic, pretty quiet, and ambiance. Can't beat ambiance."

"Think I can sell ambiance?"

"You went to hotel school."

I considered that for a moment. I could picture new business cards and a promotional web presence offering people Old Florida—before theme parks, strip malls, and chain restaurants. We could cash in on the vacations of forty or fifty years ago. Beach, sun, local dining, orange blossom perfume, roadside stands selling fruit. Maybe the aqua could even stay.

"And we have a pool," Rita added, probably misinterpreting my silence for a lack of ideas and attempting to help me out.

"We're Old Florida," I said.

"I know."

"I mean it. We can package The Gull and sell it like that."

"You don't mean sell it, right? You mean advertise it. Or should I start lookin' for a job?"

"Advertise it. Fill it with tour groups smothered in nostalgia. We'll be busier than ever."

"Think Carol and Mike will go for that?" Rita asked.

"Why not? They wanted me to make improvements without changing a thing. Since this motel is already stuck in the 1950s, it's perfect."

If I could combine a marketing strategy with some packages, I could make an effective case for my business skills. I tried to do a quick calculation of cost versus return. I was going to need a spreadsheet and some analysis tools, but it just might help me get off the waitlist for the manager program.

"I think you might be doing a zig when the rest of the town is investing in a zag," Rita commented.

I glanced around the dated lobby, trying to see it in a new light. A flicker of yellow through the condensation-fogged sliding glass door reminded me that Dalton Longfellow was waiting with his clipboard. Maybe this was a great opportunity to sell an old, but new, idea.

"It's crazy. And that's why I love it," Rita said. "Hit the pool deck and talk up the old fart you got waiting under the umbrella. I'll bring out some Old Florida lemonade in a minute when I get all these broads in the limo and out of here."

****

Maybe the idea's simplicity was its greatest asset. I sat in front of the office computer at ten o'clock that night. Technically, I was waiting up for the limo that would bring a dozen manicured, massaged, drunk, and happy women back to their first floor rooms to sleep it off. I'd had Maria leave them extra ice and complimentary water and snacks before she left to go home to her kids.

I flashed back to the courses I'd taken on branding and advertising for my business minor. What message did I want to send about The Gull Motel? How could I package and sell what I had without changing it? Opening a desktop publishing program, I played with free online clip art. Palm trees. Orange blossoms. Alligators. Water-skiing? Maybe. Any picture that said 1950s or 1960s Florida ended up in a slideshow.

After an hour of picture-hunting, I poured a glass of wine and sat back to watch the images scroll automatically. I hoped a combination of wine, color, and repetition would cement the new image of The Gull in my mind. Glancing at the clock, I poured a second glass. The limo would be at least another hour. Maybe a whole lot longer, depending on how much fun they were having. Tulip was asleep under the desk, her nose on my bare foot.

Old Florida scrolled before me, blurring ideas of coconuts, sand, sunshine, and bikinis. The mash-up

74

started to congeal into an image of The Gull as the gateway to an old-time beach vacation. I pictured myself in a red bikini with white polka dots standing at the entrance to a vacation from my grandparents' era. I smelled oranges and coconut-scented sunscreen in my imagination.

It was a beach blanket movie, but it was a return-on-investment dream. I could sell what I already had with a little networking and an advertising campaign. I leaned forward and fiddled with an image on the screen. A palm tree shading a roadside fruit stand staffed by a woman in a broad hat. Perfect. Muted colors, a little patina, and a swooping seagull was the new image of The Gull Motel: Gateway to Old Florida Vacations.

Genius. And I still had half a bottle of wine left.

Movement in the doorway caught my attention.

"Don't want to sneak up on you," Skip said. "I know you hate that." He held up a bag from a downtown restaurant we'd visited twice when we were old enough to be attracted to each other but too young to know what to do about it. "Brought you a late dinner. It's only chicken strips and fries, but it's gotta be better than what you've been cooking in your room."

Tulip's head came up, her nose registering food. My nose and stomach were equally interested. "Come see this," I said, motioning him over to my computer screen.

Skip set the food bag on the desk within temptation distance. He leaned over me from behind, smelling faintly of sawdust. He wore no shirt as usual, the Florida evening retaining the heat of the day. Even in the air-conditioned office, he smelled like the warm outside evening. My body began a slow simmer without him even touching me. I was glad I had already done my thinking for the evening, because Skip tended to permeate my brain cells.

"What am I looking at?" he asked. I wanted to suggest he look down my tank top, but I had to keep my head in the game of revitalizing my beach motel. And if I knew Skip, he was already looking down my tank top.

"I'm thinking of re-branding The Gull so I can keep it the same but bring in more business. Just like my aunt and uncle asked."

"They asked you to bring in more business?"

"Nope," I said. "They asked me not to change anything but said I could try new things. I can only think of one way to do that."

"Re-branding? Are you changing the name?

"Nope, it'll still be The Gull Motel."

"Getting rid of aqua blue and seagulls? No more vinyl in the lobby and palm trees in concrete pots?" he asked. He didn't wait for me to answer. "Great idea. I'm trying to get rid of that same fifty-year-old feel at my bar."

He refocused on the computer screen and leaned even closer, brushing his chest hair over my bare shoulder and lighting a fire that started to spread. Something about Skip made me want to forget I had anything else to do.

But I did. I had a motel's image to revitalize.

"This picture looks old-style. I thought you were re-branding for the new crowd," he said. He pulled a box of chicken strips from the bag, offered me one and took a bite out of another one.

"What if I did the opposite?" I asked.

He looked at me skeptically, picked up my wine glass, and took a sip.

"That was mine."

"I know, but you weren't drinking it at the time. And I think you've probably had too much already."

"I'm serious about capitalizing on the Old Florida thing. Instead of tossing out what we have, what if we go with it and play up that 1950s and 1960s Gulf Coast feeling?"

"I thought that feeling was dead. People want chain restaurants, air conditioning, and theme parks. Water slides. Room service."

"Not all of them."

"They want those fancy circus acts, three-tiered swimming pools, shiny bars, and perfect green golf courses."

"What if they don't? How about the nostalgic ones who want to go back to vacations they took when they were kids?"

Skip finished off the wine in my glass and picked up the bottle I had in one of the extra room ice buckets.

He poured a glass and took a drink, staring skeptically at my computer screen.

"Like to know where all these nostalgic people are," he commented. "They're not busy fishing—at least not with my dad's fishing charter."

"Maybe they're waiting to be enticed by my new ad campaign," I said.

"Maybe they're stuck in a queue line in Orlando." Skip poured a box of fries onto a napkin and shoved it toward me.

I ignored him. Rita thought it was a good idea, Dalton Longfellow from the Florida Retired Traveler's Agency got excited and drained his lemonade when I told him about it. He wanted to write up a series of articles on the revitalization of Barefoot if I'd give him exclusive access. He angled for a few free nights lodging and I decided it could be a great investment. If Skip McComber wasn't on board, I'd survive without him. Unless I needed a toilet fixed or a sliding door put back on its track.

"Already opened a facebook page for The Gull," I said, attempting to change the subject. "Tried to find Harvey's Pirate Emporium, but it didn't exist."

"Not called that anymore. I'm going with Skip's Beach Shack."

I hit him with a sideways glance. "Beach Shack sounds pretty old school to me."

He shrugged. "People like old names, but they want it to look new. It's the great paradox."

The lobby door creaking, multiple car doors slamming, and a whole lot of giggling and raised voices came at just the right time. Skip could take his criticism back to his Beach Shack bar and leave me alone. When tourists started rolling into my parking lot and leaving their nostalgic dollars all over town, he'd be thanking me. For now, he could stop drinking my wine and revving my hormones, and get out of my office.

Skip strolled toward the ruckus in the lobby. I followed him, quickly counting heads to make sure all twelve of my Girls Night Out party had made it back from the spa and bar tour of Barefoot Key. Most of them were recognizable as the same women who'd left hours earlier, but there were subtle changes. Fresh highlights, professional makeup liberally applied, blouses unbuttoned a little lower, color and glued-on sparkles decorating their nails.

They walked a little looser, weaving across the small lobby floor. And they were louder. I don't know if alcohol actually causes temporary hearing loss, but these gals were making sure they could be heard.

Especially as they cat-called my shirtless neighbor until he retreated through my office and out a back door. Serves him right, I thought, as I tried to herd the pampered and drunk dozen toward their block of rooms. I was glad Rita had wisely blocked off the rooms directly above and beside the party. Because they didn't look like they were ready to call it a night any time soon.

Chapter Six

My inadequate supply of hot weather clothing had surrendered by the fourth day of my vacation. Still operating in starving college student mode, I'd soldiered on anyway wearing the same sloppy shorts and tops for weeks.

"Clearance sale next door at the Sunshine," Rita said, lifting her eyes from the computer reservation system to cast a disapproving glance at my outfit. "Saw it on the way in," she continued. "Some cute tank tops and skirts. Might have some new flip-flops that'll fit ya."

"So you're saying—"

"I'll man the motel while you go shopping. Right now. You've been here three weeks already, and since it looks like it'll be a lot longer, I can't keep my mouth shut much longer."

The Sunshine Souvenir Stand had only one owner and operator in all the years I'd been visiting. When I was little, I thought the woman behind the counter, Jeanette, was probably about my parents' age. However, looking at her now, I couldn't assign an age. Her hair was still dark by some magic of youth or chemical intervention, her skin less lined than most women in Florida because she'd spent her sunny days inside the shop.

"Hoped you'd be over when you saw my sale," she said. "Can't wear that college t-shirt any more, huh?"

"Rita sent me."

She smiled like we'd just exchanged a law of the universe and agreed upon it. "There's a woman who dresses to show her assets. Maybe I could help you do the same."

"That's what Rita suggested."

"You need color. You got pretty brown hair and I think you're finally working up a bit of a tan. How about these?" she asked, pulling tank tops in coral, orange, and yellow from a clearance table.

I owned nothing in the hibiscus explosion of color range, so there was zero chance of wardrobe overlap with these shades.

"Price is right," I said, wondering if I had the upper body to pull off a tank top. My arms were fairly toned, but not enough to distract people from my lack of ammo in the bra department.

"End of season sale," Jeanette said.

"Slow over at The Gull, too," I said, browsing the nearby racks for something subtle to pair with the bright shirts. "But things will pick up closer to Thanksgiving and Christmas. If I'm still around to see it or not."

"Not so sure I'll be around," Jeanette said, her tone taking the sunshine right out of the souvenir stand. I hesitated a second, trying to decide if I knew her well enough to pry into that remark or if I was more neighbor or friend-of-the-family league.

"Truth is," Jeanette said as she fussed with a rack of swimsuits and glanced around her quiet shop, "I'm thinking of selling out."

"This place?" I asked, feeling like a kid who found out her best friend next door was moving to a different city and she'd have to share a locker with somebody else. "Why?"

"Have you looked around? Things aren't what they used to be in Barefoot Key."

"I know some places have closed—"

"Some? Line'em all up and it's about every other place."

I thought of the three of our businesses—Sunshine Souvenirs, The Gull Motel, and Skip's new place whatever he planned to call it—all lined up and tucked away on the north end of the strip. If one of us went, would we all domino?

"Does someone want to buy you out?"

She shook her head. "Not on the market officially yet."

My relief was short-lived.

"But I think I better sell while I have half a chance. A few years ago, a real estate company bought up some places and found out they weren't so valuable. Had to sell them at a loss not long after that."

I barely had to dust off my business minor to know what that probably did to other property values in the area.

"They left town, but I hear there's another real estate wanna be around, buying up properties again. Maybe gonna develop them."

"So you think they might want your shop?" I felt like I'd accidentally swallowed a bug.

"Maybe. And maybe I ought to take advantage of the possibility before we go through another round of buying and selling that leaves us all in the tank."

I hauled my bag of clothes back to The Gull, but the bright colors didn't send much warmth my way. The idea of a long-established business right next to the vested interest of my family's motel was more snowstorm than sunshine. I wondered if Skip knew the souvenir stand was on the skids and how deeply he'd invested in a bar that could potentially lose value like the tide going out.

I didn't have to wait long to find out. After lunch, I figured there was no harm in wearing a new outfit. This represented a huge departure from conventional wisdom for me. Wearing new clothes without washing them first was right up there with trimming your toenails in public in my former fussier days. However, living on the Gulf Coast in a beach motel was taking effect.

My hair was braided, my toenails painted, my thighs exposed, and my tank top brightly-colored.

"I like it," Rita said. "Skip's coming over to check on that outlet behind the desk that doesn't work. Maybe you could offer him something nice as a thank you."

I gave her the look that says *that service is illegal in Florida and most other states.*

"I was thinking a cold drink under an umbrella on the patio," she said.

"Good idea."

Skip did his electrician thing with a little meter and put a piece of black tape over the outlet effectively declaring it dead.

"I'll bring a new box over later and fix it right," he said.

I pulled two beers from the office fridge and dangled them in front of him. "It's after lunch. And I owe you."

"For the record, I'd drink your beer even if you didn't owe me."

"I know. I'm saving you the guilt this way."

He used the edge of the counter to knock off the bottle cap. "Thoughtful," he said.

I sat under the only truly shady part of the patio, a place where the combination of umbrellas and overhang made a circle of shade. Skip pulled up right next to me, probably taking advantage of the limited respite from the sun but also sitting close enough to invite conversation. His thigh touched my thigh and created enough spark to fix that broken outlet.

"Nice outfit," he said. "Saw Jeanette had a big sale over at the Sunshine. Maybe I should get a new shirt."

In the weeks I'd been in Florida, Skip had been shirtless every single time I'd seen him. I wandered back through years of memory and tried to picture him without his chest exposed. Not one image came to mind. It was entirely possible he didn't own a shirt. I finger-pointed his bare chest and made a sarcastic face. Skip shrugged and tipped up his beer.

"Did you know Jeanette was thinking of selling her place?" I asked.

Another shrug.

"Really," I said, thinking he didn't see the magnitude. "She says maybe she should sell it before there's another round of real estate investing gone bad. Worried properties values will drop again like a few years ago."

"Never recovered," Skip said. "That's one reason I was able to buy the Pirate Emporium. But I'm mortgaged to the edge of my seat. If my property value drops fifty bucks, I'll be upside down."

"Is that what happened to other businesses in town?"

"Rumor has it. Beware of real estate companies offering high prices. I guess those poor bastards lost their shirts, too, because they pulled out and we haven't seen a sign of Sunny Dreams Real Estate in two years."

"And now another company's looking to buy?" I asked. Skin tightening along the edge of my face and a steady thrum of a pulse in my neck made me think something wasn't right. Maybe I was just worried about The Gull somehow being threatened by any talk of value loss, selling out, or foreclosure. Although I didn't know much about my aunt and uncle's financial state, I knew the mortgage on the Gull had been paid off for years. My parents had often talked about how Mike and Carol could sell it off and live well in retirement from the proceeds. Perhaps that was before property values headed south.

"I've heard, but haven't seen it yet."

"Someone should try to do something," I said. "Having closed shops and restaurants isn't good for anyone."

Skip eyed me over his beer. "No kidding," he said.

"I'm serious. Maybe there's some kind of loan or grant the city could get to help keep up these properties. Save them from going under or selling to the lowest bidder."

"Wouldn't know about that. I'm busy trying to keep my bar from washing out to sea on the boatload of money I've borrowed."

Despite the shade and my skimpy clothes, heat hovered over me and made me itchy. "Maybe I'll check it out," I muttered.

"Have you heard from Carol and Mike? Any idea how long you'll be around?" Skip asked.

It was probably an innocent question, but it sounded like an accusation. Like since I was leaving anyway, maybe I should leave local problems to the locals. Maybe I read too much into it.

"Long enough to get online and do some research. And play hostess at the chamber of commerce event in a few days."

Skip ignored my huffy tone like a mom ignores a tantrum. "Long enough to go on a date with me?"

Two questions came to mind: did I want to go on a risky date with Skip and did the invitation have anything to do with my new skin-showing outfit? Despite my claims to intelligence, it turns out I'm as susceptible to vanity as everybody else is.

"On one condition," I said, capitulating to hormones. "You have to put on a shirt."

He picked up my beer and polished it off. "Do I have to leave it on?"

Chapter Seven

Dalton from the Florida Retired Traveler's magazine—Old Farts as Rita called it—put away another sandwich and downed his third wine sample.

"Glad you came along?" I asked.

"Um-humph," he mumbled, mouth full.

I eyed the slack camera hanging around what little neck he had.

"Any good pictures for the magazine?"

Judging from his reaction, I think there was a good chance he'd forgotten he was supposed to be working. I gave him a free room for the night and a VIP pass to the Chamber of Commerce *Welcome to Old Florida* event. Figuring it would be great publicity, I didn't mind him tagging along.

"Sunset's not far off," I said. "Might be great lighting now to capture some photos."

He handed his empty plastic wine glass to a passing waitress in a bikini and sarong. Two dozen cheerleaders from the local high school were putting in volunteer hours tonight as servers. They got to show off their toned midriffs, flirt with patrons, sample the food, and earn a generous donation for new cheerleading uniforms. It was part of my job to make sure they stayed away from the booze.

"Suppose you're right. This article might really jazz up the November issue. Get me an editor's spot if I do it up right."

I was thinking the article would book hotel rooms and packages at The Gull, but I had no problem with Dalton piggybacking his dreams with mine.

Dalton took off his lens cap and focused on the row of food vendors in colorful tents right along the water. I took advantage of his distraction and slipped into the crowd.

And it was a bonafide crowd on a sultry early October evening.

Despite general lack of enthusiasm for my "Old Florida" theme, the Chamber members had no other ideas. Mine catapulted over thin air to the top of the list and we rolled with it. Temporarily employed gals like me burdened with student loan debt had to sacrifice pride for small victories.

Bikinis and sarongs on waitresses, colorful tents serving Florida themed food and drinks, some old tourist signs, a giant petrified fish, and 1950s beach music made the ticket price a bargain. Hundreds of people had turned out for the event. Of course, my favorite prop was the Gator in a Gown statue resurrected from storage. I doubt I made any lasting friends by insisting the Gator be exhumed from the city hall basement, but it was a hit at the party.

A middle aged woman manhandled three adult children into position in front of the statue and aimed her cell phone camera at them. They were probably in their early to mid twenties, about my age.

"Got one just like that from when you were little," she said. "It's an old Polaroid, but I love it. Gonna frame this one next to it." She looked much happier with her photo than her kids did. They dispersed to food tents and I was left alone with the life-sized alligator wearing a chipped red ball gown. I always view alligators as masculine. It's irrational and makes this guy a cross-dresser, but I couldn't help my naïve habit of assigning gender based on looks. I think all rabbits are female, another obvious error but I can't help it. I'm savvy about other stuff.

I toyed with having my photo taken with the dolled up gator so I could send it to my mom. She had an old Polaroid of me with that statue, too. Lots of family vacations were right here in Barefoot Key. Without even realizing it, I'd grown up living out the "Old Florida" theme I was trying to sell now.

LeeAnn waved me over to her booth. After plenty of encouragement—much of it from Maria who claimed to have had a dream about LeeAnn serving Fish Tacos at The Great Wall of China—Leeann decided to try the commercial waters by getting a space among the food vendors. From the size of her line, I judged it a success. She gestured for me to bypass the line.

"Can you believe this?" she asked.

"It's not the Great Wall, but I still think you're doing all right. And I'm already worried I'll need to hire a new maid when you become the Fish Taco Queen of Florida."

"I like the sound of that," LeeAnn said, "But don't worry. I'd still come visit you when I'm food royalty."

"That's what they all say."

"Some of us mean it. Like Skip. He still comes over everyday like he still works there even though he's living the dream next door."

"I should try to talk him into being at least part-time on the payroll."

"Smart idea," LeeAnn said. "You should go honey up to Skip to seal the deal." She scrunched up her lips and raised both eyebrows. "Like you haven't sealed it already," she said, her lips turning up at the edges.

I abandoned LeeAnn's taco stand and headed toward Skip's Beach Shack. Although he'd been a vocal opponent of bringing out the Gator in a Gown statue, he had the giant old pirate from Harvey's prominently displayed in front of his tent. Over seven feet tall and dressed in classic cliché pirate attire—striped pants, red coat with turned back cuffs and dozens of shiny gold buttons, an eye patch and a tri-corner hat—it was a tacky tourist attraction standing guard over the hooch line.

Telling myself I was not navigating directly toward the pirate and its owner, I headed down the line of vendors. But I wasn't fooling anyone. I wanted to razz Skip about his statue and revel in the success of my Old Florida theme. I'd never been to one of these Chamber events before, but I'd heard about them. And it seemed to me tonight's was a huge relative success. I wanted confirmation.

I searched for someone else wearing the peach colored polo shirt embroidered with the Chamber's logo like I was. It wasn't sexy, but I'm a team player. All the members wore this uniform and acted as hosts for the party.

I should have watched where I was walking. That would have been a more hostess-like move. But I was on a collision course with one of the cheerleader waitresses and a tray loaded with shrimp and cocktail sauce. Bright red cocktail sauce. And I didn't even have a chance to swerve.

Like Black Friday shoppers wrangling over the last TV at Walmart, we hit the ground. In her defense, the cheerleader waitress held the tray aloft over our tangled bodies on the sand, but that just heightened the drama as I watched the slow tip and slide. I knew what was coming. After a lifetime of hiding behind brainy glasses and avoiding girls blessed with boobs and hair confidence, I was at the mercy of one of them.

I didn't really blame her for letting the cocktail sauce slide my direction and not hers. She had a lot more money in her hair and bikini than I did in my ponytail and polo shirt. Plus, I had my glasses on for safety.

Just before the big splash—mercifully it was a lightweight plastic bowl containing an astonishing quantity of cocktail sauce—my vision focused on a single object. It could have been desperation, but I'm sure that was Skip McComber running toward me, his expression conveying perhaps shock and definitely amusement.

This was a hell of a display for a gal who prides herself on being savvy.

The sauce, cool compared to the warm evening air, spattered my neck and shirt. It oozed through the fabric and dampened my bra. One of my ears was clammy with cocktail sauce.

A hand grasped mine, pulling me to my feet.

"If you really wanted to do the Old Florida theme, it would be better to wrestle an alligator," Skip said, pointedly looking at my cocktail sauce covered chest. "More action than taking down a cheerleader. Crowd would love it."

The cheerleader in question reached a hand toward Skip as she ogled his impressive biceps and forearms. In deference to health codes and food service, he wore a yellow t-shirt advertising Skip's Beach Shack. And he completely ignored the cheerleader, leaving her to roll to her feet and slink off with her empty tray.

"Aside from the obvious," he said, gesturing at the wreckage of my polo shirt, "any damage done?"

He held me at arm's length, apparently not wanting to share my food stains.

I sighed. "Never better. But I have to run home and change."

"And miss the party? You could...uh...maybe brush some of that off?"

I gave him a look that would win a sarcasm contest.

"Or find something else to wear. I think they're selling Barefoot Key t-shirts at one of these stands. Or I could fix you up with one of my bar t-shirts. Even has an old-time graphics scheme." He pointed both index fingers at his t-shirt which did, indeed, have an old-fashioned beach shack and palm trees inside a giant tequila glass. Like a Florida-styled snow globe.

I hated to confess I was soaked all the way through. I needed a new bra or the red sauce would permeate a fresh shirt like ketchup through a bun. Maybe I could get a red shirt and hope nobody got too close.

We walked a few paces toward Skip's busy drink tent and I found my deliverance in something I thought I would never wear.

A tube top sundress. No bra required or expected. Colorful. Old Florida. Okay, maybe 1970s Florida, but it was still old. And it was available in a huge range of shades and patterns.

"Maybe I'll get one of those," I said.

Skip followed my pointing finger and his eyes lit up.

"Wouldn't mind seeing you in one of *those*."

I rolled my eyes and cut off into the dress tent, not bothering to see if Skip followed me.

"Something not too revealing," I told the lady working the counter. Although she had fifty pounds on me, she was shoved into a tube top sundress in a bright orange hibiscus pattern. She looked all right. Maybe I could pull this off, too.

I arranged myself in a tropical blue dress with splashy yellow flowers, hoping people would focus on the pretty pattern instead of my inadequacies in the boobage department.

"Not bad," the clerk said. "Wouldn't have thought you had a figure under that godawful polo shirt."

I handed over twenty five bucks, slid into my flip-flops, shoved my wrecked clothes in a plastic bag, and sashayed from the tent.

Skip was right where I'd left him. He did *not* look at the yellow flowers. Instead he moved in and kissed my bare shoulder, giving me goose bumps everywhere.

"You taste like shrimp sauce," he said. "Very sexy."

I thought I was trampy in this dress, but I'd take sexy. There were still several hours of party to get through and I couldn't let being taken down by a cheerleader then subsequently scrunching into a tube top with a skirt wreck my game.

"I need a beer," I said.

"Coming right up."

I shook my head. "Think I'll head over to the beer tent. I'm supposed to be sort of supervising. Or hosting. Or something."

"But you're incognito now. You could get away with anything. Get drunk, sing karaoke, have sex with one of the vendors. Preferably me."

"Tempting," I said.

"And you don't have to worry about the beer tent. My dad's working it."

I tried to picture Jude McComber responsibly checking IDs and somberly cutting people off after they had too many.

"Since he's an alcoholic," Skip continued, "you've got a professional in charge there."

"Your dad can't be an alcoholic," I said.

"Why not?"

"Because he owns a business. He's a local personality," I protested. "And he has a beautiful name. I think Jude is a saint's name."

"Drunks can own stuff and have personality. And I bet there have been plenty of saints who hit the bottle."

I thought about Jude McComber's secret life. Hell, maybe it was no secret. Just because I didn't know it doesn't mean it's classified. Since I'd shown up at The Gull over a month ago, I'd found out how little I knew about anything.

"In his defense, he doesn't drink on the boat. Never did. But he's a crappy businessman. Everything went downhill when he took over the charter boat from my granddad."

"So you bought a bar."

"Like the irony?" he asked.

"I'd still like a beer," I said. I thought getting a little sloppy might bring everything into focus and make me forget about my outfit.

"Offer of drinking, karaoke, and sex still stands, but I have to get back to work. People are knocking back my barefoot mixers like they're gonna disappear with the sunset."

When I reached the event sponsored beer tent, I had no trouble finding Jude McComber. He stopped me at the entrance, holding out a hand and rolling like a wave on the sea. He peered intently at my face.

"I'm supposed to ask your age," he said.

He did not look like he was in any shape to be in charge.

"I'm fifty-two years old," I said, highly doubting he was paying any attention.

"Proof?" he asked.

I cocked my head and sucked in a deep breath. Which was a mistake because the booze vapors coming off him put me over the legal limit by just breathing.

"Do you know who I am?"

He focused on me again. "Sure. I...uh...didn't recognize you in that," he pointed at my trampy 1970s tube top dress. "Savvy Thorpe," he said like a revelation had come from the Almighty.

"You're drunk," I said.

"Yep. But not crazy like the rest of you chamber nuts. I don't think even a nice shindig like this is going to get us all out of the crapper."

I wanted to protest. It was such a success, this evening by the gulf shore with crowds, wine, color. How could the business community of Barefoot really be going downhill at the rate it appeared to be? Certainly the location, if nothing else, should keep it afloat.

"Come on," I said. "This is great. Maybe it's a new beginning for Barefoot Key."

"Or a really pretty ending," Jude said, polishing off a plastic cup of beer.

I considered my answer. Jude didn't seem like a mean drunk, just a skeptical one. And maybe he had good reasons. "Your fishing business is going all right, isn't it? The package deal we put together with The Gull already has some bookings. You fill up your boat, I fill up my motel."

"Not gonna do me a helluva lot of good if the marina I operate out of sells out."

"Is it going to sell out?"

He looked at me like I was a little girl who thought the upside down fish in her tank was just sleeping. "See that tent over there?" He pointed to the multi-colored tent operated by Sandshore Realty and staffed by a few sharp-looking salesmen. I'd planned to stop by there this evening and see what they were going to do. Maybe someone should warn them that the last real estate company that "invested" in property here ended up losing their shirts and selling low, dropping values for everyone and leaving an ugly stain on the whole town.

"Since you're not wearing a Chamber shirt, maybe you should go ask them what the hell they think they're up to," Jude suggested.

"Are they up to something?"

He tipped his cup over and appeared to be considering its empty condition, the gesture removing any credibility from his thoughts on the local real estate market.

"Everybody's always up to something," he concluded, his words slurring.

"Maybe they have good intentions. They see a great opportunity for growth in a cool beachside community."

"Smart girl like you shouldn't dress like that," Jude said. "Makes you gullible."

I didn't get a chance to disagree because a flash went off in my face.

"You look great in that Old Florida dress," Dalton said, oozing closer and checking out the digital photo on the screen of his camera. "I'll put this picture in my magazine article for sure." He looked at me closely, an expression of concentration on his face. "I think my Mom had one a lot like that in the 70s."

That was my motivation for escaping the beer zone and heading for the tents. They were colorful, so I thought I might blend in better. Perhaps people would mistake me for a tourist or a local looking for fun.

The Sandshore Realty tent was set apart from the others and distinguished by having strangers in business casual instead of locals in dressed up swimwear. It looked like a crystal bowl among paper plates. Maybe I was lowering my standards the longer I hung out in my beach motel on the gulf coast, but I was starting to think paper plates were all right.

A salesman wearing a button-down and trousers handed me a brochure. "Have you heard of our company?" he asked. His nametag identified him as Robert.

"A little," I said, not interested in showing my hand and not being really untruthful. What did I know about this company?

"We're a small real estate company looking to grow by investing in wonderful beach towns like this. Places with character that need a little money to push them into the next century."

"That's quite a goal," I said.

"A good one. These little towns have plenty of attractive features," he said, glancing over my outfit. "And we're always looking for people to join our team of associates."

I was being recruited? After thirty seconds of conversation?

"Here's some information about our company. My number's on there if you think you'd like to hear more."

I was pretty sure I'd heard enough already but was in the lucky position of having nothing to lose. "Do you think your company can reverse the damage done to property values in Barefoot by the last real estate company that invested and lost its ass?" I said.

"We have nothing to do with that company," he said quickly, his tone losing some of the manicure it had before.

Maybe it was my outfit making me feel so salty. I stuffed his brochure down the front of my elastic dress and sashayed off. Picking fights with strangers is no way to enjoy the sunset.

Chapter Eight

My aunt and uncle had called faithfully every few days to give me the progress report on the reformation of crazy Aunt Gwen. Except for today. They'd already called three times.

"We should be glad it's hitting on a Sunday night," Rita said. "Not a whole lot of reservations to cancel that way."

"So we're totally empty?" I asked.

"Except for you. You can come to my house and hunker down if you want."

This was my first official hurricane and the last thing I wanted to do was ride it out alone. Growing up in Michigan, we had the occasional tornado threat, but never an all-night howling wind with storm surge potential. What did I know about handling that? And what would I do to protect the motel?

"Of course, if I were you, I'd spend the night in Skip's storm shelter like he offered. Hurricane or not, most women I know wouldn't pass up a night with Skip

McComber. And it would probably just be the two of you since he doesn't have any employees and his folks will be at home."

I considered the wisdom of locking myself up with Skip. Our history was a pretty clear indication of what would happen. The knocking in my chest where my heart was supposed to be was another indicator. Over six years of sometimes friendship, sometimes tension, occasional action, and always attraction had weathered me down like a rock in a stream. Spending a steady five weeks here with him next door was temptation my college education had taught me nothing about.

"Probably not a good idea," I finally said.

"Don't see why not. He's available. You're available. What's the problem with you two?"

"I'm supposed to be focusing on The Gull."

"And?" she asked skeptically, hands on hips.

"And Skip messes up my focus."

Rita shut down the computer and locked the file drawers under the checkout counter, handing me the keys. She switched the outside sign to *No Vacancy*.

"Skip said he'd come over and get the hurricane plywood on as soon as he's done at his place," Rita said. "We've got boards sized and stored for all the beach side windows. Used them plenty of times before. Just have to put them up."

"What else?"

"All the patio tables, chairs, and umbrellas go in the shed. Hard to fit them all in, but it can be done when we get all the plywood out. That comes out first."

"Thanks," I said. "I don't know crap about preparing for a hurricane. Think there's a chance the whole thing will miss us?"

Skip slid the patio door over and stepped in.

"Sure," Rita said in answer to my question. "It'd totally wreck the orgasm they're working up on the news channel, but it could turn south or stall out and we'd just get some tropical weather out of it. Happened before."

"I'm hoping for that."

"Hate to ruin a good orgasm," Skip said.

"I bet it happens all the time to those guys on the weather channel," Rita said. "Mother Nature is a tease."

I stayed out of this conversation, figuring I should maintain some dignity as the manager of The Gull. A gust of wind bracketed the patio door and I shivered.

"Just an early band," Rita said. "The big stuff will hit later. Are you sure you want to stay here?"

Skip raked me with a look. "You can't stay here alone."

"But I don't want to leave The Gull. My aunt and uncle trusted me with it."

"They don't expect you to stop a hurricane," he said.

"But what if the power goes out and I have to do something important?"

"Like what?"

"Like unplug stuff. And get junk out of the pool. And use flashlights or something."

"You also have to flush the toilets once every hour so they don't overflow," Skip said, his expression serious.

I almost thought he wasn't kidding for a minute until Rita laughed.

"You're not helping," I said.

"But I'm just about to. I pulled all the boards out of the shed. I'll start screwing them to the window frames while you two haul the patio furniture into the shed."

We battled wind gusts and horizontal rain showers for an hour as we did what we could to secure the outside of the motel. Rita and I toweled off and tuned in to the Weather Channel for a few minutes on the lobby television, but they were stuck in a loop providing no new information. My aunt and uncle called to tell us they were following the storm on television, too, and urged us to stay safe.

Rita shook the water off her coat. "Maybe it'll go south of us and we'll just get some wind and rain," she said encouragingly. "I'm headed home. I can't leave my dog alone any longer. She'll chew the arm off the sofa if it gets real ugly. You watch out for yourself here and don't forget Skip's offer of his walk-in cooler. You might need it."

Rita stopped in the door and turned. "Mind if I take Tulip home with me? My dog'll be happier with a playmate and it gives you one less thing to worry about."

If Tulip was any kind of a service dog, I'd insist on keeping her nearby. But she was more talented in the entertainment and mischief department. Sending her home with Rita was an easy choice. I clipped on her leash and handed her over closing the door behind them.

I prowled around the lobby and office, checking on windows. I hauled one of the smaller potted palms inside. If nothing else, it was company. I got a beer from the small fridge in my uncle's office and parked myself on the aqua vinyl sofa to watch the Weather Channel until either the storm passed or I went insane. I started to feel lonely. Vulnerable. Stupid.

I still had half a beer left when the door leading to the first floor set of rooms wrenched open.

"Just checking on you," Skip said. "Staying here alone isn't the smartest thing."

"Coming out in the storm isn't so smart either. And anyway, I'm prepared."

"Do you have any food and water?"

"Vending machines are stocked. The guy came yesterday."

Skip gave me a look I'd seen the slower kids in school get from teachers all the time.

"That's your big plan?"

"I can live on pretzels and cookies for a few days if I have to. I even got cash and quarters to have ready."

"You know those don't work when the power's out. Right?"

I focused on the latest weather map, hoping it would somehow erase my stupidity and replace it with either drama or good news. I'd take either one.

It was the same thing they'd been showing us for hours, and Barefoot Key looked to be directly in the path of the storm. Unless you believed an alternative model the ecstatic forecaster flipped to briefly. I had the impression he wanted to see Barefoot Key get it. Maybe I was just being sensitive as a result of feeling like a total dumbass.

"I thought I'd break the glass in case of emergency, like if I need a Milky Way or a Diet Coke. I'm in charge of the place. I can do that," I said.

Skip sat next to me on the vinyl couch and watched the screen, chin in hands. I could tell he was shirtless under his rain slicker. That wouldn't be sexy on most men, but something about it made me want to peel off the outer layer and see what Skip had to offer me.

I thought it was a reasonable idea considering I might die in the impending hurricane.

"Where are you staying tonight?" I asked.

"Next door. Don't want to leave my bar, and I have a pretty decent shelter I already invited you to."

"Why don't you want to leave your bar?"

He sat back. "Because it's the first thing I ever owned. Hell, it's the only thing I own. Aside from a very used Jeep."

"So you see why I don't want to leave The Gull."

"Nope."

"I feel responsible for it. Like you and the Pirate Emporium."

"Beach Shack. And it's not the same thing. You don't own The Gull."

I wanted to argue, but the television screen beeped and a scrolling message in a fiery red box grabbed our attention. The message could be paraphrased like something out of Dante's Divine Comedy. *Abandon all hope and kiss your ass goodbye.*

"I wish you'd lock the doors, get your coat, and come next door with me. I've got food, water, and flashlights. And it's going to be a long night."

I hesitated.

"I promise I'll come back over here with you at first light to assess the damage," Skip said. "I've worked for your aunt and uncle a long time. They know hurricanes, and they would think you were out of your mind for trying to be a hero."

A building-shaking gust of wind hit The Gull on the beach side and I gave up the fight practically before the first battle. I remoted the television off, grabbed my purse from the office, and unplugged the computer.

"Right behind you," I said.

The wind had continued to pick up, buffeting me as soon as I hit the doorway. Skip wrapped one powerful arm around me and steered me the short distance to his bar. Whipping sand stung my face and I felt like I was half floating. Bundling me through the door, he closed and barred it by shoving a heavy table in front of the wood door. He leaned on the bar while I took a glance around. Despite construction supplies and a general state of confusion, the bar retained much the same look I'd grown up with.

"I remember coming over here a few times on vacation. Used to get a Coke before I was old enough to drink."

"Remember old Harvey?"

I nodded. "What happened to him?"

"Retired. Signed over the paperwork, handed me the keys, and took off for a vacation home in Tennessee. Guess he'd had enough of hurricane weather."

"Can't blame him," I said. "What made you decide to buy this place?"

"Needed to do something. Never told you, but I've got a business degree, too. Community college, just a two-year thing, but it got me thinking. Fishing isn't going anywhere, and I always had a soft spot for this place."

"Why?"

"Dad used to bring me here. Probably the reason Harvey was willing to sell it to me. Didn't want it to go to some outsider."

I thought about that for a minute. "Am I an outsider here?"

"Nope. You're related."

Somehow, I found that encouraging.

"I have some good memories of Harvey's," Skip continued, absentmindedly wiping off the bar surface with his wet raincoat. He grinned at me. "Had an awesome date a while back that started here."

I didn't need to ask how that ended, flattering myself that he meant me. Not that I knew anything about the rest of his love life, but I liked to think I'd ruined him for all other women after our one night together.

A strong gust of wind bracketed the windows and howled between his building and the end of The Gull. Despite my determination to be brave, I shivered and zipped my hoodie a little higher.

Skip's eyes were on me, not the worn bar now. "Show you the shelter," he said, draping an arm over my shoulders and turning me toward the kitchen. He led me through a kitchen that was missing most of its appliances, gaping holes where they had once stood.

"Major need to modernize those. No idea how they ever passed health inspections," he said. "That was a no-choice big expense and it's a real pain in the ass. They keep backing up the ship date and I can't move on with construction in here until I get appliances. Luckily I have one functioning oven and I got a carry-out pizza earlier today. We can heat it up later when we get hungry."

"What kind of pizza?" I asked, even though I was in no position to be picky.

"Your favorite. Bacon and black olives."

So Skip had been thinking of me when he picked up that pizza. "You don't like black olives," I said.

"We're in a weather emergency. I'll pick them off."

Skip's walk-in cooler wasn't any more glamorous than advertised. Aside from a case of bottled water and two sleeping bags rolled out in the middle of the floor, it was mostly a graveyard of old junk. A battery-operated lantern provided enough light to check the corners for spiders—a necessity if I planned to get any sleep. Not that I planned to.

He motioned me in and pulled the heavy door shut.

"How will we get out?" I asked, panic raising my voice twelve decibels higher than it needed to be in the small space. "I've seen this in movies, people getting trapped in coolers. Happens all the time."

"Only to idiots. This door is also keyed from the inside and I—" he paused dramatically, making a big show of digging in his front pants pockets and forcing my eyes down there "have the key right here."

I sighed. I hated to admit how much safer I felt with Skip, especially since he'd prepared with a key and sleeping bags and pizza. You can't buy that kind of confidence.

"So now what do we do?" I asked.

Skip slow-smiled and leaned against the cooler door. "Taking suggestions."

I pulled out my cell phone. "Any reception in here? I could track the storm with my phone."

"Exactly what I was thinking," he said in a mock serious tone. "Pretty sure the reception is better the lower you go."

I gave him a look.

"I'll show you," he said. He shrugged out of his raincoat and tossed it over a box. Then he sprawled out on a sleeping bag, crossing his arms behind his head so I could admire his bare chest.

I attempted to look disinterested, glancing at my phone and trying to update the radar. A yellow bar told me my network was unavailable. Great. I was hunkered down in a hurricane wondering if and when it would hit. There could be tornadoes, too, and how would I know when to put my hands over my head if I couldn't see the Weather Channel?

My eyes strayed to Skip's front pants pocket that bulged with a rectangle the size of a phone.

"I know what you're thinking," he said.

"I'm sure you don't."

"You're wondering if the phone in my pocket has any service."

"Maybe I was admiring the bulge in your pants," I said, hoping ridiculous with a trace of truth was the right tone.

"Easier to admire from down here. And you can test the theory."

I hesitated. Stuck in a cooler with Skip who was half old friend and three quarters crush mixed with one all-the-way fling. The math didn't add up and that makes me crazy. The air pressure from the storm combined with the enclosed space made my head feel too light. Getting down on the floor was the safest move. It was the savvy choice.

I knelt on the sleeping bag next to Skip as a half-measure. A test. I glanced at my phone so he would know my move was purely scientific. Not surprisingly, altitude had nothing to do with reception.

"I could text Rita and ask for updates. I bet that would work," I said.

Skip nodded, never taking his eyes off me.

I sat on my sleeping bag, one of my feet straying onto his as I tapped in a brief message to Rita, hoping it might slide out of the cooler on a slice of bandwidth.

"Feel better?" Skip asked.

I nodded.

"Did you tell Rita you were locked in the cooler with me and that's why you can't see the weather radar?"

"No."

My phone beeped. It was a message from Rita. All it said was, "Does Skip have his shirt off?"

It beeped again. Another text from Rita. "Sure you want interruptions?"

Skip grinned. "Updates already?"

I idled my phone to save the battery and set it on an overturned plastic crate.

"Always good to have Rita on your side," Skip commented. "I'll have to tell her tomorrow how much I appreciated it."

I crossed my ankles and sat back on my elbows. Skip rolled up on one arm, edging closer and giving me his full attention.

"Hope you're not scared."

I shook my head. "Nope. Just worried about The Gull."

"Nothing you can do about it."

"But I'm still allowed to worry."

"I could take your mind off your problems," he offered.

I knew he wasn't bluffing. His hands had talent. He had proven that over years of maintenance magic at the motel. There had been ironclad proof last spring when a night out with a few friends over my last college spring break had turned into multiple hookups. My friends met some local boys they hardly knew while I ended up in the sack with someone who'd been raising my awareness and heart rate for as long as I'd known him.

Skip unzipped his sleeping bag and spread it wider. He reached over and unzipped mine. I sent him a questioning look.

"Getting comfortable. Gonna be a long night."

I scooched onto his open sleeping bag and let him pull my unzipped one over me. It was cold on the concrete floor. I reasoned there was no sense freezing, and our minds would be sharper if we were both warm. I might even be able to take off my hoodie eventually if I thought I could stay warm in just my tank top. I applauded myself for my logical thinking.

Right until Skip pulled off his work boots, settled in beside me, and stretched out full length against me. This was no place for logic.

"Much better," he said.

As his guest, I didn't think it was my place to argue. There had been many a lonely night in my cold twin bed on campus. I'd had plenty of time to fantasize about Skip.

It had been a hell of a vindication to find out he was just as tasty as I'd been imagining for years.

But now was no time to think about that unless I wanted to sample him all over again.

I inched backward, leaving a little space between us as I toed off my shoes. "I'm guessing you've ridden out your share of hurricanes," I said.

"Uh-huh. Used to be scared when I was little. All that loud wind. My dad would always try to rush out and check on his fishing boat and mom would be in a panic until he got back."

"How often did this happen?"

"About once a year we get a serious tropical storm, major hurricanes only a few times in my life and they usually just grazed us."

I thought about that and hoped it would be the case with this one, too.

"Hope this one does too," he said.

I smiled. I was already used to Skip voicing exactly what I was thinking.

"How about you? Any big storms growing up in Michigan?"

"Tornado sirens once in a while, but never a direct hit in our town. Snowstorms are more likely."

"But not scary," he said.

"Not when you're a kid and you're looking at a few days off school."

"Sounds like fun. I've never played in snow."

"Never?"

He shook his head. "Nope."

"Not even on a vacation?"

"Vacation is right here," he said.

"You don't know what you're missing," I said. "Sledding, building snowmen, getting ice and snow down the back of your neck until you finally remember to put up your hood." I shivered thinking about it.

"I prefer heat." Skip moved in, securing the sleeping bag over me and holding it in place with one long arm. His warmth and scent enveloped me and thoughts of the cold melted away.

Chapter Nine

I couldn't pinpoint the exact moment when I decided having sex with Skip McComber for the second time in my life was a good idea. I think the idea took root when I accepted his offer of a shelter for two for the night. I'm pretty savvy, but my powers of resistance are no greater than anyone else's. A dish of chocolate candies won't last five minutes in front of me, and I'd already exhausted my Skip resistance completely in the month I'd been in Barefoot Key.

If I was going to die in a hurricane, I was going out satisfied.

His kiss did not surprise me. I felt it coming even with my eyes closed. It was the kind of kiss that erased my sense of fear about the hurricane outside. It removed any sense of discretion I might have felt upon being slowly stripped of my clothing. The kiss eradicated any common sense.

And I was glad to see it go. Here snuggled in sleeping bags riding out a storm, there was no room for any senses that weren't directly involved with bodily pleasure.

We repeated the dance of flesh on flesh that we'd experienced six months ago, and my heated remembering of it wasn't exaggerated. It was the kind of sex that makes you quiver just thinking about it when you least expect it. Like standing in the grocery store line or crowding into an elevator.

I'd thought about Skip a lot in the half a year that had passed. Every time I did it, I'd glance around hoping no one could guess my thoughts.

Now, it was going to be twice as bad. Maybe three times if we had to be hunkered down all night.

Rita beeped in with a text update just when we'd dozed off, oblivious to the outside world and the winds bracketing the bar beyond our shelter.

"Winds weakening, eye turning inland, worst hitting south of us," the text said.

I texted back a brief thanks and relayed the news to Skip. We were in total darkness, the lantern switched off to conserve batteries just in case.

He yawned. "Still going to be strong storms on the outer bands this side of the storm. Better stay put. Unless you want me to heat up that pizza."

I shook my head. I was happy to burrow into a Skip shelter and forget everything. Tomorrow, I could claim it was the storm. Just in case anyone asked me to explain myself. I seriously doubted anyone would. Rita wouldn't even have to ask. Except maybe she'd enjoy some salacious details if we weren't too busy picking palm trees out of the swimming pool.

For tonight, I just wanted to enjoy doing something that had nothing to do with being Savvy.

Electronic beeping registered somewhere on the edge of my thoughts but I ignored it. I kept my eyes closed, hoping it would go away. Skip stirred and I heard his cell phone flip open and shut, but I didn't even bother to ask.

"Text from my dad saying same thing Rita's did," he muttered.

For a moment, it occurred to me that I didn't have to expose my situation to Rita's gossip since Skip was in communication with his dad the whole time, but I gave up that train of thought. Rita would have found out anyway, and it was probably good that I'd have someone to talk this over with in the morning.

We awoke hours later. Skip rolled over and flung an arm across my chest, pinning me down and leaving a stream of warmth where his bare skin met mine.

"How long could we hide in here before someone came looking?" he mumbled.

I considered it, wondering how much damage we'd find when we emerged. "No one's looking for me," I said. "My relatives are all in another state."

"No matter what we find when we go outside," Skip said, his voice low and tremulous in the darkness, "this was the best night I've ever had."

I wanted to think of an intelligent response, but I settled for the bone-deep truth instead. "Me too," I whispered. "Unless you count spring break last year."

Skip chuckled and pulled me tighter.

I sighed. "I hate the thought of going out there, but my aunt and uncle are going to want to know right away. They were probably up half the night."

"Think I'll probably dig out my insurance policy first. It'll soften the blow," Skip said.

"Does insurance cover hurricane damage?"

"Sure does. That's what I'm counting on."

"Counting on?" I sat up, pulling the sleeping bag over my exposed skin and trying to get oriented. I was naked, stiff from sleeping on concrete, and beginning to feel the morning after questions coming.

Damn that hurricane.

"Hurricanes can sometimes be your friend," Skip said, stretching long arms over his head, not caring how much skin he was showing. "I might get a new roof out of it. I could use that."

"Oh. Never thought of it that way."

"The Gull might end up with a facelift sponsored by your friendly agent if the damage is bad enough."

"I don't want damage," I said, a sinking feeling fully replacing the satisfaction of the earlier hours.

"Doesn't matter if you want it or not. You get what you get."

If I were on a playground swing, this would be the point where I realized I'd blissfully gone too high and now the swing was wobbling out of control. I had to slow down or risk a dangerous jump. I hate those decisions.

I reached for my clothes in the dark shelter and started to pull them on, not caring that I was tugging the covers around with me.

"Want me to turn on the lantern?"

"Not yet," I said quickly. I wanted to get my clothes on and see what my motel looked like. I wanted to regain control of the weather, my property, and especially my nerves.

"Say when."

I zipped my jeans, slithered into my tank top and covered up with my hoodie.

"When."

Skip switched on the lantern and lay back watching me. He was totally naked and didn't care.

"You seem upset."

"Hurricane," I said.

"Probably more of a tropical storm by the time it hit us."

"Whatever."

He sat up and looked me over. "No one's going to blame you for damage to The Gull. Even smart people can't stop gale winds."

"I know."

"So why are you putting on your shoes and edging toward the door?"

"Curiosity."

He sighed. "Wait for me."

Skip pulled on jeans and boots and rummaged in his pocket for the key. As he opened the door, my heart was on a railroad track, racing over an abandoned bridge. We walked up two steps and into his bar. It looked exactly the same as yesterday. Aside from the boarded windows allowing almost no light, nothing had changed. The power was out, but that was no surprise.

"So far so good," he said.

The good news lasted until he opened the beachside door. Attempted to open. Sand was piled so high he had to pour his weight behind a hard shove just to open the door a few inches.

"Other door," he said. As we crossed the bar to the parking lot side, I was picturing every door on the first floor of The Gull barricaded by a mountain of sand.

"You've got the patio and the pool deck in front of all your doors. You'll probably be fine," he said, guessing my thoughts as usual.

No resistance from the other door stopped us, and we stepped into the early morning light of the empty parking lot. Skip paced out several feet and looked up at his roofline. My attention was fixed on The Gull next door.

A potted palm lay on its side across the patio door.

Sand swirled in piles and small hills on the pool deck.

One loose board from the edge of the roof swung like a pendulum in the wind. It looked like an abandoned Wild West town from a movie set. But it was all intact.

"Damn," Skip said. "No new roof for you."

"I was happy with the old one."

"All the window boards held, don't even think that patio door is damaged."

"Good."

"Maybe," he said. "Might have been nice to replace it. It's older than you are."

"Part of the charm."

"You talk a lot about the old charm. Starting to think you actually care about this place."

"Of course I care about it," I said.

"Thought you were building your resume and biding your time until you can get out of here."

The outrage rumbling in my chest had a number of possible causes. Damn near all of them had something to do with Skip McComber.

I tried to keep my voice steady. "You think I only care about the motel because I can get something out of it? That's a hell of an insult."

Skip held up both hands in front of him like he was trying to stop traffic. "You said yourself you needed to do something to get into hotel training camp and demonstrate business savvy."

I rolled my eyes at his use of my nickname. It felt like a violation of the self-incrimination amendment.

"So I wasn't so sure how much you were attached to The Gull," he tapped a finger over my heart, "in here."

I stared at him, not able to come up with a suitable answer, not knowing how much what he said was the truth.

"Guess maybe I underestimated you," he said.

I let out a deep breath. Too much drama over the past hours was messing with my reason. I needed to start making a list of damages and costs. It would restore my equilibrium for at least the time being.

Skip was probably thinking the same thing. He leaned out and sighted down the side of his bar. "My building looks okay. Just got a lot of sand and water to sweep out."

"I wonder how downtown looks," I said. I thought of the people I'd met at the Chamber of Commerce meeting, all of them dependent on their businesses and local tourism. A storm like this wasn't catastrophic, but it put a serious hitch in the account books for a few weeks. And might make it tough to make the monthly bills. With bills of my own, I could sympathize.

"Will it put your construction project back very much?" I asked.

He shook his head. "I'm mostly doing inside stuff right now anyway. Didn't have much in the way of outside renovations planned. Kind of like the old look, except for the pirate statue."

"You don't like life-sized statues?" I asked.

"When I was a kid, I always hoped the Gator in a Gown statue would get washed out to sea," he said, grinning. "Or at least knocked over. My buddies and I were often tempted to graffiti it, but granddad would've killed us."

"I love that statue," I protested. "It's got character." I glanced around my pool patio littered with small pieces of debris. "This is a mess."

"Barefoot Key's been through this plenty of times," Skip said. "We'll be fine."

From his tone, I couldn't tell if I'd been initiated into the storm survivor's category or reminded that I was an outsider. For the hundredth time, I tried to imagine my future. Here in Barefoot Key? Probably not after my aunt and uncle returned. Working at the Grand Chicago in a crisp navy blue suit? That was the plan. It just seemed a little windblown right now, too.

And I had no idea what Skip's idea of our future was either. We just hooked up for the second time this year. The difference was that this time I wasn't here on a one-week break. We'd have to figure out what the next day and the next would bring for our relationship. At least until I could hand The Gull back over to its rightful owners.

Skip's body language was unreadable, and his expression pensive as he shaded his eyes and looked up and down the strip of motels, shops, and bars along the beach. I followed his glance and decided nearly everyone looked to be in the same shape we were. Messy, but still around. A few other people were walking around their property looking alternately up and down, assessing.

For a distraction, I walked around the end of The Gull to check out the parking lot. I didn't look to see if Skip followed me or not. Maybe we both needed processing time.

Water pooled in quivering puddles, some sticks and leaves were shoved up against the room doors. A used tire had rolled in and lodged in the front flower bed crushing the yucca plant. The aqua sign with the sea gull stood as still as ever. The neon lights advertising vacancy or not didn't work, but I didn't see any damage. When the power came back on, we'd probably find it was strangely fine. It had apparently withstood a few storms in its half century.

Rita rolled in and Tulip jumped out the passenger side window without waiting for the car to stop.

"Holy shit, we got a mess," Rita said. "Better get going on it."

I swung around to see what Skip would say, but he was gone. He had his own mess to clean up.

"Hope you got a little sleep last night," Rita said. "Although you probably had a lot more fun if you didn't."

Chapter Ten

"My nephew Ralph is pretty useless, but at least he's a warm body. And we really need someone for crap jobs like cleaning up storm junk," Rita said.

"Two questions," I said. "Will he work for minimum and can he start today?"

Rita laughed. "Hell, he could have started last week. He hasn't had a job since he graduated from high school last June."

"Very encouraging," I said. "We don't have to untrain him."

"Figured you'd see it that way. I'll get him in and show him the ropes if you want to do something about the fall fishing package guys we got coming in later."

"Deal."

Although the hurricane had only rolled through two days ago, people were already going about their normal routines. Tourists drove through town. The trash truck emptied the dumpsters. The doors at the souvenir stands were open. Fishing boats were going out to try their luck in the calmed waters of the Gulf.

A group of six men were scheduled to come in this afternoon to put up for the night. They'd go out with McComber charters in the early morning to see what they could reel in. Six rooms that would have been empty otherwise were booked and maybe I could hook them for another night if the fishing was good. My account books would have a sunny side and demonstrate I had the business savvy people seemed to think I did.

I hoped my fishing charter guys would have smoother sailing with the elder McComber than I was having with the younger.

After our night in his storm shelter, we'd both been busy. The truth is, that wasn't much of an excuse. We'd both practiced some serious avoidance. I didn't know if we'd try to surpass our last record of six months, but we had a start. Over the past forty eight hours, I'd vacillated between showing up naked on Skip's doorstep and showing him the door if he bothered to come nosing around again.

Maria came in the lobby and sat on the vinyl couch, swinging her feet up and taking a break.

"All done," she said. "Sand swept, rooms spiffed up. And I'm in no hurry to go home."

"Got a good babysitter?"

"My husband's home for the week. The trucking company he works for had storm damage at its central warehouse, so they're not moving any merchandise until they get it repaired."

"Don't you want to go home and spend some time with him?"

Maria pursed her lips and sucked in a deep breath. "Do you think I need any more kids?"

Not being an expert in that department, I kept my mouth shut. I printed out the guest list for the night, only six names on it.

"Is it weird that all six men have the same last name?" I asked. "I hope they're not a cult or something."

"All separate rooms?"

"Yep."

"Brothers," Maria said. "Probably still fight if they have to share a room."

"I don't have any brothers. And I'm obviously no expert on men," I said.

Maria assessed me with a serious look from her feet-up position on the aqua couch. "I think things are going to work out for you just fine," she said.

"Got a crystal ball?"

"Not exactly. But close."

"How close?"

Maria swung her feet down and came over to the counter, leaning on it with both elbows. She glanced around and spoke just above a whisper.

"I know things," she said. "Things that are going to happen."

I put down the list of fishing brothers and gave her my full attention.

"Maybe it's what they call a sixth sense," she continued. "I've always had it to some degree, but it seemed to get a little sharper with each baby I birthed."

I laughed, trying for levity because I was getting a little weirded out. "Your kids probably can't get away with anything."

She flicked her hand. "All mothers have that sense. Kids are predictable. What I'm talking about is something else. Last year when that big sinkhole happened up by Tallahassee, I had a dream about it the night before. And that man in Tampa who robbed all the churches on the same night? I saw that coming in a vision."

"Have you told anyone about this?"

"Only a few people, people who share the gift."

"There are others?"

Maria glanced around and leaned closer, lowering her voice even more. "Ever since I got a computer, I found a way to put my gift to some good use."

"I'm almost afraid to ask."

"Stock trading. You can do it on the internet."

I'd minored in business. I knew this. But Maria was still a mystery.

"Exactly what are you doing?"

"It's called day trading. You have to be good with predictions and you gotta be fast. It takes dedication."

"I've heard about it," I said. Quite a lot. But I didn't have the spare money or the nerve to try it. I looked Maria over carefully. Blue housekeeper's uniform, curly dark hair cut short, dark complexion overlaid with a tan, big brown eyes. I wouldn't have picked her out as a day trader, but what did I know?

"So how are you doing this?" I asked.

"I formed a group. We all go to St. Mary's. Some of us work days, some afternoons and nights. We take shifts sharing an account and our...uh...."

"Intuition?"

"That's a good word for it."

"Are you making any money?" I asked. It sounded too good to be true.

Maria looked down at the countertop and several seconds passed. Finally, she looked me in the eye. "I'll tell you that we're looking for a good cause to spend our money on, but that's all I can say. We swore each other to secrecy, most of our husbands don't even know."

I raised my eyebrows at that.

"Men make a mess of things," she said, her face relaxing into a smile. "But not all of them. Which brings me back to you. I had a vision about you before you got here. My dream started out with the old Gator in a Gown statue in a flowing white dress, but it shifted around and when it finally ended, it was you in a wedding gown."

There was absolutely nothing I could say in response. Except that I'd always felt a certain connection to the Gator statue. Maybe Maria the day-trader just provided the answer.

And maybe it was a cautionary tale about getting too much Florida sun.

****

Turned out, Maria was right about one thing. The six Texas fishermen were brothers. Three tall, three short, no in-between. Even during check-in, I could see why they couldn't or shouldn't share a room. Having never had a sibling or a brother, I've missed out on the joy of elbowing, fighting for first in line, and bickering that seems to go with the territory.

These Texans were experts. I suspected Jude McComber would need every ounce of his personal equilibrium to keep them all afloat early the next morning. Rita was still trying to instill job training in her new maintenance man, so I manhandled the Texans and handed over keys to six rooms that were not adjoining. I wasn't taking any chances with a stray punch or any roughhousing tearing up my motel.

My motel. I tried out that expression a few times as I sucked in air conditioning in the now-empty lobby. The longer I breathed Gull air, the more I felt it becoming part of me. Had I been in training to run The Gull all my life? Maybe I should have spent all that tuition money on something else. Like a library full of first editions. Or a convertible.

I slid the frosted door open and stepped onto the pool deck. The six Brady brothers were all there, drinking out of a cooler they'd rolled in. They waved me over. I hesitated, so one of the tall ones opened the lid on the cooler and gestured at the goods inside like he was a game show host.

He'd make a good TV personality. Long lean body, chiseled jaw. He's what I thought of when I thought "hot Texan."

"Think it violates the innkeeper's code of conduct to drink with guests?" I asked.

"I believe it's a requirement south of the Mason-Dixon Line," the tall hot one said. "Especially when you own the place."

One of the brothers tossed a rubber ball for Tulip who retrieved it with a level of enthusiasm that suggested she was in the game for the long haul. I guess I hadn't played with her as much as Uncle Mike probably did. Tulip and I would both be delighted when my aunt and uncle rolled back into town. Whenever that was going to be.

"I don't own it," I said, choosing a chair in the middle of the group and using the edge of my shirt to twist off the top of my beer bottle. "Just babysitting it until my aunt and uncle get home from vacation."

"How long they been gone?"

"Over a month."

Six pairs of nearly identical eyes swung toward me. All the brothers gave me a questioning look.

"How long were they gone on their last vacation?" This question was from one of the short brothers.

"They've never taken one before."

Now all six men made sounds that were variations on the theme of "um-hmm."

"They're coming back," I said, sounding a little defensive. Maybe desperate.

A tall and short Texan leaned toward me and clinked their beer bottles with mine. "So what are your plans for the place?" the tall one said. "Not much to look at, but it's got character. Plus, you can't beat the price with a fishing trip thrown in."

Maybe it's a sign of my general fear of failure and being found out as less savvy than I pretend, but I got all warm and fuzzy at approval from visiting fishermen. Could be the alcohol talking, since my reputation for not holding my liquor is better documented than my college transcripts.

My bolstered ego lasted another thirty seconds until Skip swaggered onto the pool deck. He was over six feet of tasty man with exposed abs and intense eyes that always made me wonder which side of the balance sheet I was on.

Arms crossed, he surveyed the impromptu drinking party on my pool deck. He didn't look happy.

"Need something?" I asked.

Skip cast around the deck like the answer to my question was somewhere under one of the aqua umbrellas.

Since he didn't answer, I filled in. "These are the Brady brothers. From Texas. They're all going out with your dad on the charter boat tomorrow." I turned to the brothers six. "This is Skip McComber, his family owns McComber's Fishing Charters."

The brothers all put down their beers and got up to shake hands with Skip. Those guys had manners. Skip, however, looked like he'd walked into a formal wedding wearing flip-flops. Awkward.

"You'll find his father, Jude, is much more talkative," I said. Skip shot me a look.

"Long as we catch something," one of the Bradys said, "conversation is optional."

Another odd silence. I took a deep breath of man-smell. Six different scents mixed with the pool's chlorine and the salty Gulf. But there was another one of familiar spice coated with sawdust that held my attention.

One of the Bradys offered Skip a beer. He shook his head.

"Computer trouble," he said, addressing his words to me and sounding like he'd just found something he'd been looking for since last Christmas. "I've got computer problems."

"Try unplugging it and waiting two hours," a tall one said. "Works every time."

"Not that kind of problem. Stupid spreadsheet program," Skip said.

I didn't have to be a college grad to know Skip was asking me for help, or at least using it as an excuse, but I didn't rush to let him off the hook. He could ask nicely. Maybe even beg a little.

"I was hoping," he said, lowering his voice and moving closer. "You might come next door and help me figure it out."

"You live next door?" one of the Bradys asked.

"Not exactly," Skip said.

He didn't elaborate, so I played hostess. Which I guess I technically was since we were all knocking back brews on my borrowed patio. "Skip bought the pirate bar next door and he's fixing it up. He used to be the maintenance man here at The Gull. He can run the pool pump, get doors unstuck, and get Barbie dolls out of toilets." Skip's look was somewhere between puffed up and pissed off. "But he can't run a computer I guess."

"I can run the computer. Just don't know how to make all the columns do what I want on the spreadsheet thing," he said defensively. "Guess I'll figure it out since you're busy."

"We can move this whole party," a tall Brady suggested. "Wouldn't mind seeing your bar."

"It's not open yet."

"So we'll roll our own cooler over." They all stood up, picked up their bottles, and headed for the bar. From their smooth transition, I'd guess they'd moved a party before. One of the short ones grabbed the cooler handle and towed it behind him.

No one could doubt the Bradys from Texas were easy to get along with. As they poked around Skip's bar and offered their genuine praise of the place, I tried to get to the bottom of the spreadsheet problem. Skip seemed torn between showing off his bar and squeezing close behind me at the makeshift desk in his unfinished office space.

"Thought I might get you alone," he said.

"Plenty of chances for that."

"Seemed like a good chance."

"You know, I almost thought you were faking your accounting problem just to get me away from my drinking party with six attractive men," I said, rolling my eyes at Skip when he tried to feign innocence. "But you have this ledger so screwed up, I don't even think you could fake it. You need a bookkeeper. Desperately."

"You're hired."

"I already have a full time job."

"So do I, but you have me over there all the time fixing stuff. Seems like this is fair play."

I thought about that for a minute. I had some showers running slow, a doorknob that came off in LeeAnn's hand, and two televisions that wouldn't communicate with their remote controls. Skip couldn't identify red ink from black and would be in a heap of trouble if an auditor ever sniffed his way to the former pirate emporium. We could be good for each other.

"Deal," I said.

Chapter Eleven

All I could imagine about the article in the Old Farts magazine was that it would be sweaty. Partly because Dalton was writing it, but mostly because the air conditioner in the lobby and office at The Gull was out to lunch the day Dalton came for a final interview. October on the Gulf Coast is not Michigan-sweater-weather, and I was itching to yank off the polyester polo shirt. I had only set aside my new tank tops so I would look semi-professional for Dalton Longfellow.

Rita's nephew hauled in a toolbox and pretended to prod around, but he was pretty distracted by his cell phone. Probably updating his status on some social network. I'd guess it would say something like "can't fix this lame a/c" or "working sucks."

I needed a pro. Or I was never going to survive pouring on the charm and serving up lemonade to the editor-hopeful across my desk.

"You're a sight for sore eyes," I heard Rita say to whoever slid open the glass door in the lobby. I knew who it was.

"You always say that," Skip's voice said, carrying into my office and making my itching worse. My attitude was in the shitter. But I was sweating out pleasantries and calling in favors.

Skip poked his head in my office. Shirtless. Of course. Wearing cargo shorts and work boots. And smiling.

"Hear you need me," he said. He nodded toward Dalton, acknowledging him and giving me a look that suggested he understood my predicament. "You know part of the charm of these old beach motels is their quirkiness," Skip said. "Just like guests, you don't always know quite what you're going to get."

"Can I get you to fix the air conditioning?" I asked.

Skip opened the control panel on the front of the wall thermostat. He smiled. "Another nice thing about these Old Florida places is you've got people who've worked in'em for years. Know all the ins and outs." He

159

ducked into a recessed office closet and snapped open a metal door. "So you know just who to ask."

A click from the closet was followed immediately by a rush of air from the vent. It was warm at first, but the coolness brushed me before I could even complain.

"Gotta get a picture of this," Dalton said. "Shirtless man saves the day."

I resisted the compulsion to roll my eyes, focusing instead on the cold air now blasting me. I wondered if putting up with Dalton's dorkiness was worth the potential free publicity from his magazine. I'd already sunk three nights free lodging in his visits to Barefoot. For all I knew, he was stringing out his "research" to get free vacations. Hell, maybe he didn't even work for the magazine.

Dalton snapped a picture of Skip and looked giddily at the image on the back of his digital camera. My guess was he'd gotten it for his last birthday. "I'll put this picture next to the one of you in that tube top dress thing," Dalton said.

No amount of frigid air conditioning was going to make that okay. "I'd prefer to focus on the motel instead of me," I said. "I'm only temporarily running this place," I continued, shooting a look at Skip and wavering between wishing he'd leave and hoping he'd stick around. "So it's really about the motel, not the person behind this desk."

"Like a human interest angle," Dalton insisted. "I'll choose a bunch of pictures to put in. Depends on my editor, too. You'll just have to be surprised when it comes out."

"When do you think that might be?" I asked.

Dalton looked at his old-man walking shoes. "Not sure. The higher-ups at the magazine don't seem to recognize my talent. I'm hoping this article will change their minds." He rubbed his hands together. "I can't wait to see my name next to the headline *Barefoot holds Key to Old Florida*. See what I did there? It's a pun."

I smiled politely, imagining he got the same kind of encouragement from his mother.

"Why don't I show you our new website," I suggested, reverting to business savvy and hoping Skip would get bored and take his ripped abs next door. "I think the branding I'm working on says it all."

Dale scooted his chair a little closer and leaned into the monitor, shoving his glasses into position on his sweaty nose and making me appreciate Skip's ability to know which lever to switch.

In addition to pushing all my buttons, he was a handy man to have around.

****

When the lingering sweat smell was all gone, eaten up by cool air conditioning, I could think again. There was some office work I could do if I wanted an excuse to stay inside for the afternoon. I moved a few piles around on the desk, feeling at loose ends with my life, my position as temporary-ish manager of The Gull, my love life, and whether or not I should get another one of those slutty dresses.

"Heard about the Sunshine?" Rita asked, sliding into an empty chair by the office door and crossing one bare leg over the other.

"The shop?"

"Uh-huh. Sold out," she pronounced, obviously waiting for my reaction.

I took a slow breath. Rita had time on her hands and I hoped stalling would make what I feared go away. "You mean she sold all her merchandise?" I asked. "Good for her. I picked up some nice clothes."

Rita gave me a look.

"People know a bargain when they see one," I continued, trying to smile but knowing I was being a pain in the ass.

"Guess that real estate company knows a bargain when *they* see one," Rita said.

I gave up trying to hide from the truth. "What do you think the real estate company will do with her place?" I asked, feeling like I'd swallowed something large without chewing first.

"They told her what she wanted to hear, if you ask me. Said they liked what she had going and promised to keep something like her shop in the same location."

"That sounds nice, but they have no obligation to do that unless it's in the contract. When they own it, they can do whatever they want," I said. "I'm glad they don't have enough property to do anything that'll compete with us."

Rita gave me the look again. "You don't think they're gonna come knocking on our door next?" she asked.

"The Gull's not for sale."

"The Sunshine wasn't, either, until rumor got out that Sandshore Realty was paying better than people had a right to expect based on their last property valuations."

"My aunt and uncle don't have a mortgage, and they have never said a word about selling. As far as I know, they plan to stay here until either they turn to dust or The Gull does."

"Huh," Rita said. "Never know what people are gonna do until they do it."

The heavy feeling in my throat wasn't any better. "Is this happening anywhere else in Barefoot? Anyone else suddenly selling to Sandshore?"

"Hard to say, people are pretty close-mouthed about their business until it's obvious. Or they're friends like the Sunshine."

"But this same thing happened a few years ago, right?"

"Uh-huh," she said, slipping off her sandals and examining her pedicure. "Bunch of places sold, folks moved on, and they're either still empty or sold out for less. Shitty deal for everyone, especially, I guess, those dumbasses in the real estate company that bought'em and lost money or got stuck."

"Businesses aren't in the habit of losing money or making bets they think won't pay off," I said.

"That what they taught you in college?"

"Some of it."

"Cause that's not what we're seeing around here. Guess Barefoot Key is the exception."

The bell on the lobby door jingled and Rita returned to the desk. I heard her out there going through the ritual of checking someone in for the night.

I typed Sandshore Realty into a search engine on my uncle's desktop computer, a nagging suspicion lingering in my mind. I knew enough to know companies only bet on losers when losing is their goal. Why would a real estate company nose around and buy properties on which the last company lost money? I reasoned that it could be the *buy low, hang on, and sell high* later philosophy. If so, there would probably be records of Sandshore Realty's previous dealings. Somewhere. Looking for property transactions would be a lot more helpful if I knew where to start.

The flyer from the smooth guy at the tent was wrinkled from having spent the evening down my sleazy dress front, but it was still there under the desk mat in my temporary office. I slid it out and read it over for the first time. The website listed on the front was only window dressing. The site had glossy pictures, an "about us" page that was as informative as a redacted CIA document, photo-shopped pictures of company executives, and a form to fill out to contact them.

There was no way I was going to learn anything about Sandshore Realty the easy way.

A small button at the bottom of the page caught my attention. Careers. I remembered Robert's suggestion that I join their team, but had passed it off as a direct result of my glorified tube top dress. A person could learn a lot about a company through the application process, and it was certainly a believable reason to ask questions.

Rita popped back in the office, the lobby quiet again. She lounged on the corner of the desk, killing time while she waited for a few more people with previous reservations to roll in. I closed the page I had on the screen because I didn't want to share my half-brained plan with anyone. Especially someone who'd tell me it was half-brained.

"Ready for a birthday party?" I asked Rita, changing the subject.

"Whose birthday?"

"Some little girl. Part of my plan to fill in the empty slots in the company spreadsheets. I'm opening the pool for kids birthday parties on weekdays. Decent revenue, not much cost for us. Put it out on social media and got two booked already."

"Nice idea," Rita said. She said it in the same way you'd tell an old lady her new perm looks good.

"Glad you think so," I told her, pulling up the party reservation on my computer. "Because I need someone to make balloon animals and do magic tricks."

Rita rolled her denim buns off the desk and headed for the door. "I have to rearrange the

167

complementary toiletries under the counter. Might need to order some extra shower caps," she mumbled as she trudged off without looking back.

"I'll take that as a yes," I called out, knowing Rita would rather scrub seagull poop off the roof than play hostess at a princess themed birthday party. Unless I let her be the princess.

Chapter Twelve

I wanted to relax and enjoy my date with Skip. It seemed like weeks since he'd officially asked me out and we both finally finished circling the idea. Sure, we'd had sex in his walk-in cooler on the night of the hurricane. But this was a date. It implied premeditation and potential commitment.

For fun, he suggested we recreate our first "date" when we were sixteen and we drove down the coast for ice cream. The weather was perfect, still hot but fading color mellowing everything into peachy coral shades, removing harsh lines everywhere.

My tank top, chosen in deference to the Sunshine, short-shorts and flip flops were all Florida style. No Michigan on my body. I even had a tan and a sun visor.

"Is this the same Jeep?" I asked.

"Believe it or not. When I got the guys at the dealership downtown to spray it all one color, I found out it looked pretty good," Skip said, draping a beach towel over my seat to cover the cracks in the vinyl.

The baby blue paint did look pretty good.

"It even runs almost all the time. Nearly a perfect record so far of getting me home from wherever I've gone."

"I'll take it," I said.

We took the same route down the coast we'd taken a half dozen years ago. This time, we were eating dinner and then maybe adding ice cream. Skip kept his focus on shifting gears while I tried not to think about what I'd done earlier in the day. My curiosity has led me down some decent intellectual paths and beefed up my savvy image a few times in the past. Today, however, I wondered if I'd gone too far in investigating Sandshore Realty.

Skip pulled into a seafood restaurant, the kind that mixes elegant and casual to the extent you're guaranteed to be dressed right for it. Not taking chances on shrimp cocktail, I ordered an innocent salad.

"You're thinking about something other than that food," Skip said.

I took a bite and tried to look enthusiastic. It was good food, but Skip was right about the focus of my attention.

"Do you always think about food?" I asked.

Skip looked up and right, pretending to seriously consider my question. Not only had he shaved and exposed all his handsome face, but he was also wearing a shirt. For added points, the shirt was not screen printed and did not advertise anything. Not even beer.

"Nope," he said. "Sometimes I think about beer. And sex. And fixing stuff. Been thinking about my bar a lot lately."

"Have you decided when your grand opening will be?"

"What do you think about Halloween?"

Still a few weeks away, I hoped I'd still be around. The news from Michigan had not been encouraging about my great aunt. Carol and Mike were doing the rounds of doctors and social workers, searching for a good solution before returning to Florida. My parents, although they weren't directly related to Carol's mother, would have tried to help, but they lived several

171

hours away in Michigan and were spending their retirement travelling. I wondered if my dad's brother Mike ever considered retiring or if he planned to go out with the sunset at The Gull.

No matter how complicated things were up north, apparently my assurances about The Gull's well-being were convincing enough to buy me more time in the driver's seat. But I had no idea how much time.

"You don't like the idea?"

"Will I need a costume?" I asked.

"That's the idea. I'm throwing a party for my grand opening. Last year, this town was dead on Halloween. Kids got candy from all the shops downtown, and then it was all over at eight o'clock. Not this year."

I ate, thinking about a possible costume appropriate for a bar grand opening. Maybe I could shimmy into a Gatsby era dress or go as one of Charlie's Angels or something. I could ask Rita and either LeeAnn or Maria to team up with me. Or not.

"How about a pirate theme?" I suggested.

"Thought about it, but not sure it sends the right message. I've spent all this time getting rid of the Pirate

Emporium look, starting with the giant statue. I think I should go forward, not back."

"Everyone around here seems to be worried about that," I muttered. The sale of the Sunshine and the empty buildings around town weighed me down. The fact that I concealed all those problems from Carol and Mike over the phone made me feel like a cheater. I couldn't have lied to their face—I lacked the skill and nerve for that—but assuring them over the airwaves seemed okay. And they had plenty to worry about already, I reasoned.

"What did Carol and Mike say when you told them about the Sunshine selling out?" Skip asked.

I didn't reply.

"You didn't tell them," Skip said, his voice edged with more understanding than criticism. His powers of mind reading were less impressive than you might think when you factor in the truth that my face is an open book. A flaw I would have to address if a job interview actually came out of the online application I'd filled out that morning for a customer service representative's job— whatever that is—at Sandshore Realty.

"If the Gull were in any danger, I'd tell them," I said.

"You mean immediate danger."

"Of course."

"Because we're all in trouble if another round of property value tanking goes on. I'm about fifteen bucks away from my equity ceiling right now."

"Maybe I should buy you dinner," I suggested, feeling relatively solvent and hoping to change the subject.

"You could," he said, smiling suggestively, "but then you'd probably expect sex later if I let you wine and dine me."

"That's how it works, sailor."

As it turned out, I didn't buy dinner. I just bought ice cream at a stand a few miles closer to home as the sun totally faded. But I got my reward in sex anyway. Having an attractive and willing man camping out in the bar next door seriously uncomplicates the logistics of a physical relationship.

But logistics were part of my overall problem long term because I didn't know how long I'd be needed to run the Gull and I was still on the waitlist for January in Chicago. The longer I stayed in Barefoot, though, the more the fancy hotel job started to seem very far away.

****

I hit print and ran to the printer, ready to catch and conceal what came out. The reservations system on the lobby counter shared the office printer because it was really only a few steps away.

"You in there, Savvy?" Rita called from the lobby.

"Yep," I said, still waiting for the printer to wake up and spit out my paper.

"Tulip's in trouble. Took some kid's pool toy and won't give it back. Mom's put out about it. I'm checking in a guest out here."

Torn between guarding the printer and handling the dog crisis, I hesitated. Then I heard barking and yelling outside and gave in. As I crossed the lobby, I thought I heard the printer come to life but it was too late. Maybe I'd be lucky.

"Drop it. Tulip! Drop!" I emerged from the sliding glass door, already yelling and trying to command our overgrown puppy.

Rita was right about the pool toy, but wrong about the Mom. She was pissed off more than put out. Clearly not a dog person, she was unamused by a wet yellow lab carrying a blow up dolphin in her mouth like it was a baby. Every time Tulip clamped down, the dolphin squeaked and endeared itself even more to her. The kids in the pool—including the owner of the toy—loved the spectacle, but I was obligated to intervene.

"She's a stray," I said, catching a glimpse of Skip striding over. I guess he heard the barking and squeaking.

"Lives next door," I continued. "Hey neighbor," I yelled. "Come get your dog before I call the dog catcher again."

Skip gave me a sideways glance that suggested I would owe him later. A lot. He whistled and Tulip capitulated immediately, running gleefully to my neighbor's bar. Skip opened the side door and Tulip dashed in. I imagined her visits would have to cease once he got the place going and health codes became more important. Not many bars and restaurants have a pet, and Tulip would probably steal wallets, car keys, purses, and condoms from unsuspecting bar patrons. She could get a bad reputation.

It took me a few minutes to mollify the ticked off mom, but since the dolphin still held air and floated, there was no serious damage done. I was hoping to get back in the office and grab my paper from the printer before Rita saw it.

One look at her face when I slid back through the glass door told me I was too late. She held it out to me with her trademark *what the hell is this* look.

"Must be a good explanation for this," she said, holding out the confirmation letter with my interview time and directions to the Sandshore Realty corporate office in Tampa.

"Uh-huh," I said.

The only reason I'd concealed this from Rita and everyone else was because I thought I was being completely paranoid and stupid. Not two traits I want in a lover, myself, or even a pet.

Rita didn't move. Didn't offer me the letter. Didn't offer me any way out.

The door slid open behind me bringing humid air and a scent of Skip's soap mixed with sawdust I'd come to know quite well.

"What's going on?" he asked, stopping with his hand still on the door handle, ready to make a quick retreat in case he'd stepped into a cat spat. Which is what it probably looked like.

"Skip know about this?" Rita asked.

I shook my head, torn between explaining myself fully, telling them all to go to hell, or grabbing the paper and running into the Gulf.

Skip removed at least two of those options by clicking the door shut and taking the paper out of Rita's hands.

"Job interview?" he said.

I nodded, waiting for the rest of his reaction to roll out. Rita was way ahead of him, you could tell from her expression.

"Why are you messing with this company? I don't think they're on the up and up," he said.

Rita huffed out a long, loud breath and gave him the *you're a dumbass* look.

"What?" Skip asked.

"Since Savvy's got her lips all taped together, I'll tell you what I think she's doing. Nosing around. I think she's cozying up to this company to see what their deal is."

I wondered for about five seconds how Rita guessed that, but then I remembered my open-book status and Rita's professional people reader status. She probably knew what I was thinking right at that moment.

"I don't know what the hell you're thinking," Rita said, "going down there to Tampa and wasting your time. You're not going to find out anything there that you couldn't find out searching all over the internet."

"Maybe I will," I said.

"So that's what you're doing?" Skip asked. "Really? Going on a fake interview to snoop around that company?"

I let my silence be my answer.

"Why?" he prodded. "It's a real estate company. I think they're being stupid buying properties in Barefoot when those properties obviously can't hold their value."

"Says the man who sunk the next thirty years on a mortgage for a *property* next door," Rita said.

"That's different. I'm sticking around. I'm no investment company looking to turn around properties and make a quick buck."

For a moment, I hoped they'd continue to fight with each other and leave me out of it, but that was too much to hope for. Still, I tried taking a small step backward out of the triangle.

No dice. "You're not going anywhere," Rita said. "Skip, you tell her this is a dumbass idea."

"It's a dumbass idea," he said, cheerfully complying with Rita's order.

Like I didn't already know that. Still I couldn't shake the thought that something about Sandshore Realty wasn't legit.

"I have a right to apply wherever I want. Maybe I've decided to stay in Florida instead of putting my snow tires back on." Rita gave me a look of total skepticism.

Skip's look was harder to read. We'd had no conversation about where our relationship was going, if anywhere. One thing was sure, though, if I stayed in the area, we'd have to figure out where we were going. If I headed north, the question could remain unanswered.

"I'm going with you," Skip said.

"To Chicago?" I asked, my train of thought clearly on the wrong set of tracks.

Skip's brow creased with confusion causing Rita to sigh loudly and retreat behind the front desk, slapping him on the head as she went.

"Says here the interview's in Tampa," he said. "I'll drive you."

Chapter Thirteen

"It was a good idea to require them to reserve rooms," I observed. Rita and I were trying to ride herd on a cowgirl birthday party. The cake was shaped like a pony, the girls wore pink hats, and their moms even got in on the action by dressing as several variants of cowgirl ranging from slut to slutty ranch hand. I imagine Skip's appearance halfway through the party more than justified their efforts. It was probably a disappointment when Skip removed the plastic pony from the pool filter and continued on his way next door to the Sunshine.

I was planning to go over and help Jeanette set up her clearance tent and clean out her storage closet as soon as the birthday party at The Gull settled down.

"My thought was they could use the shower and have a decent place to change, but now I'm afraid it'll just mean they stick around longer," Rita said. "That's a lot of little girls. Have to throw in the nuclear pool chemicals when they leave."

"And hose off the deck." Pink icing, laced with sprinkles and glitter, decorated the pool deck. An abandoned cowgirl hat floated in the pool sending out a little cloud of colored water where the cheap construction met the chlorine.

"We could hose off the kids, too," Rita suggested.

"LeeAnn and Maria were against the idea, and now I see why," I said.

"Can't judge from LeeAnn. She's against everything. But you might want to listen to Maria next time."

"Because she has kids?"

"And other things," Rita said.

I wondered if Maria had revealed her powers of prophecy to Rita or if Rita had just figured it out. Rita gave me a searching look but kept her mouth shut, probably wondering how much I knew about Maria's church group with the internet gambling gift.

Despite the strange contrast of the pink themed party with the aqua blue motif of The Gull, I liked it. Sure the kids were loud, the moms were a pain in the ass, and we'd have a mess to clean up. But rooms were booked and people were having fun. The heavy scent of spray-on sunscreen hung in the air, smelling like vacation.

I took a moment and enjoyed the scene at my motel. The Gull had no doorman, no valet parking, no elevator, no concierge desk. But it had sunshine, the sparkling Gulf of Mexico—whose color nearly matched the signature shade of the motel—and it had history. It was starting to feel like home.

****

The mail came while Rita supervised the pool party and I held down the ancient countertop in the office. One embossed envelope made me suck in a deep breath and hold it until I'd found the letter opener in the junk drawer. I nearly passed out by the time I got the envelope open and read the first three words.

I was in.

The manager trainee program at the Hotel Chicago was pleased to tell me that my status had changed from waitlist to official trainee. The letters I'd sent them detailing my improvements at The Gull had worked! In only a few months, I would be standing behind a marble counter in a lobby with a waterfall in the center. I'd be directing people with expensive luggage to have a nice day.

I eyed the margarita machine under the counter. Should I celebrate? I sighed. The letter directed me to respond with my acceptance within ten days. I decided to think about it tomorrow. I could celebrate when the cowgirl party left.

After the pool partiers had polished off cake and ice cream, the moms in power hauled the girls to their rooms to shower off sand, sunscreen, and sticky food. Rita decided she didn't need to guard the pool deck any longer and headed into the cool lobby to reclaim her post behind the desk. The only rooms previously booked on the slow Tuesday afternoon were the birthday party guests, but there was always a chance of a drive-in reservation.

I headed over to the Sunshine to help Jeanette. When I got there, Skip was securing the last stake of a large tent in the parking lot. Just seeing my neighbor on a ladder putting up a final clearance sign made the gravity of the situation real. I wondered what Uncle Mike and Aunt Carol would say right now if they knew Jeanette had sold out to the new real estate company moving in and making promises they probably wouldn't be able to keep. I knew I should tell them, but I hated to burden them with problems here while they tried to sort out Carol's unpredictable mother.

Jeanette handed me a marker. "Want to write prices on all this stuff?" she asked.

"Just tell me how much," I said.

"Heck if I know. Whatever you think I can get. All goes into my retirement plan along with the money I got for the place."

I wanted to ask so bad it was physically painful. If I asked Jeanette, I knew she would tell me what Sandshore Realty had offered her.

"It wasn't a bad offer," she said, taking advantage of my open book face. "I know you're curious. I would be. We all have to worry about what happens to our properties when others sell out."

"I'm glad it was an okay offer," I said.

"Still feel like a rat leaving a sinking ship," she said. "But it's a good chance for me to move on."

"You're not betraying anyone," I said.

186

Jeanette came down and leaned on the ladder. "Glad you and Skip are both here so I can tell you at the same time."

Her tone suggested storm clouds on the horizon. Skip gave me a puzzled glance and I could see he didn't know what was coming either.

"When I went to do the paperwork for the final sale and transfer," Jeanette said, pausing to straighten her clearance sign, "something came to light I forgot all about."

"Something bad?" I asked.

"Not for me, but it might for you," she looked anywhere but at us as she spoke. "Years ago, I made an informal agreement with Harvey and your aunt and uncle to let traffic go past here to the Pirate Emporium and The Gull."

"Let traffic go past?" Skip asked.

"Uh-huh."

"Wait," I said. "Isn't this a public street?"

"Not all of it. Part of it's private, came with this property. The turn off from the main road, right in front of where we're standing, goes with this parcel."

I didn't know what Skip was thinking, but I sure knew trouble when I saw it. This could be disastrous.

"We're all friends," Jeanette continued, her tone apologetic. "So we never put it in writing. An informal easement you might call it."

"But now—" I began.

"Now whoever buys this old place doesn't have any obligation to honor a friendly agreement, no matter how long it's been around."

Skip finally processed what Jeanette was saying. "So, my bar is cut off? If whoever bought your place decides to be a jackass about it, they could close this access road by cutting it off at the entrance?"

"That's what could happen," Jeanette said, the lines of her face weakening as if she was five seconds away from tears.

"And no cars could come down the street to The Gull or my place?" Skip asked.

Jeanette nodded.

I was starting to think a phone call to my aunt and uncle was something I should have done a week ago. They would have known about this easement and maybe something could have been done. Now, it was a done deal and The Gull could end up isolated from the flock.

Chapter Fourteen

On the hour's drive to Tampa, I talked myself into and out of what I was about to do. Three times. Interviewing for a job I had no intention of taking was a new adventure for me. For one thing, I had the acceptance letter in my purse from Chicago. For another, I was only going to Sandshore Realty corporate headquarters to snoop around.

At least I'd talked Skip out of going with me. Going incognito would be a lot tougher if I took along a man whose looks turned heads. Especially if the man in question also thought I was a moron for going on this interview in the first place.

The headquarters for Sandshore stood out from its neighboring buildings because of its height and its shiny newness. Glass instead of stucco or brick and ten stories instead of three made the building look like Miss America visiting a preschool of ugly ducklings. I wondered which of those two categories I'd fit into.

I parked between two vehicles with chrome and trim worth more than my whole car. Because I had only vacation clothes with me, I'd asked my parents to ship my official navy blue interview suit with matching heels. I told them I was representing The Gull at a Chamber of Commerce event and wanted to look professional. They let me off the hook without asking questions.

It wasn't technically a lie. I had represented The Gull at a Chamber of Commerce event, but I just happened to be wearing a trampy tube top dress at the time.

"Savannah Thorpe," I told the sharp-faced woman at the desk.

"One moment," she said icily.

Everything about her said knife-edge polish. Angular haircut (fresh), razor-like cheekbones (blushed on), crisply ironed blouse (mercilessly tucked in).

How anyone battles Florida humidity and stays unfazed and unwrinkled is a mystery to me. Maybe I'd learn if I stuck around.

I doubt the steak-knife receptionist appreciated it when I parked my portfolio on her counter and used both hands to shove my shirt back in my waistband and snap the car wrinkles out of my jacket.

The elastic sundress suddenly seemed very appealing.

"Right this way," knife-woman said.

The lobby was filled with windows and doors, plenty of escape routes if I lost confidence and headed for the Gulf Coast highway. I snatched my folder and steeled my resolve.

I was here to snoop, and I had to remember that.

I thought we were headed for the elevators, but the pencil skirt and heels turned down a long hallway filled with doors, institutional carpeting, and occasional alcoves with chairs and fake plants. Could Sandshore Realty really employ all these people? The doors went on and on. Maybe they weren't offices, they were there just for show. Hell, for all I knew, every janitor had his own office.

I kept my eyes open and my brain on overdrive, noting the names on the doors. Glass doors. Gold lettering. Through the doors—all closed—desks and people were visible.

The truth hit me like a rogue wave.

Sandshore Realty was not *one* company. If this building was any indication, it was a conglomerate. My mind reeled backward, gathering information and evidence from every business course I'd taken for my minor. What if Sandshore was so large it didn't even notice a little loss like the property values plummeting in Barefoot? It would be like a millipede losing a leg. No big deal. But a *big* tax write-off.

With my new working theory, I walked with more purpose down the endless hallway to a door marked Sandshore Realty Personnel. Blade-woman waved me in and edged away.

The man behind the desk shoved a drawer shut as he stood and extended his hand. "Chester Thomas," he said, smiling in a business-like manner.

"Savannah Thorpe," I said. This was an occasion for the bravado I could muster from my full formal name.

I took the seat he indicated with his free hand and put my portfolio on a fake leather chair matching my own. No idea whether I'd need it or not.

"You've come a long way for this interview," he said.

My mind rewound the one hour drive down the coast and I knew my open-book face probably conveyed confusion.

"From Michigan," he said. He pointed to a paper in his hand, presumably my resume and online application.

"Oh. I'm actually…uh…staying with friends in the area for a few weeks. Until I find a job."

"I see. And where exactly are you staying?" He waited, eyes widened, hand poised with pen over my paperwork.

I hesitated, not wanting to reveal too much.

"So we can contact you," he nudged.

"My friends live north of here. Barefoot Key. But you can use the cell number I provided on the application."

When I said Barefoot Key, his expression altered. A slight narrowing of the eyes. A twist of his top lip. Involuntarily perhaps, but something in his face suggested he'd heard of Barefoot Key. For all I knew, though, he might have gotten drunk there once. Or laid. I took a closer look at the guy. Okay, maybe not laid.

"Our company has some interests in that area," he ventured.

"I'm guessing real estate," I said. If only he knew how much I already knew and wondered.

"Of course. That's our business. How closely connected are you to your...uh...friends in Barefoot Key?"

I tried to decide what the right answer was. Maybe he hoped to hear I was interwoven so closely in the community that they could use me like a mole— assuming I had the loyalty of a rodent. Maybe he was afraid I'd be more like a canary in a coalmine and warn everyone about the write-off scheme I thought Sandshore Realty had going on.

"Not close," I said. "Just passing through and soaking up sunshine on my way to a great job." I smiled winningly. "Perhaps here?"

Chester Thomas picked up a paper. "I have your file here. Nice credentials. Not exactly real estate experience, but hotel management and business combined is a close second."

"Thank you," I said, believing that must have been an indirect compliment.

He asked me a standard interview question. Then another. And another. I began to think the interview was going well since I made it past the first few questions. *What would I do if they actually offered me a job?* Staying in Florida had its appeal. Sunshine. Skip. Flip-flops. Skip. Tank tops. Skip.

I continued to smile and give appropriate answers about my experience with customer service, managing money and paperwork, my education. Chester checked off boxes on his sheet. The clock hand on the wall swung south. It had to be almost over.

When my interview concluded, what would I do? Go right out his door instead of left? Infiltrate the employee cafeteria and nose around? Ride the elevator up and down until someone spilled the beans on the corporate strategy?

"I'll walk you to the front desk," Chester offered.
Crap.

"That's okay," I said. "I think I'll use the restroom on the way out."

Given my readable face reputation, I had no idea if he was going to buy it, but I probably profited from the male/female dynamic. It's a universal rule that men do not interfere with women on the way to the restroom. One little mention of a tampon and they retreat.

His face relaxed, the professional smile melting. "You'll find it on your right as you enter the lobby."

Dismissed. His tone as he gave the direction and body language as he turned to his computer screen told me I could go.

But I wasn't done. I had a little pride on the line here. Hadn't I dressed up and driven an hour for this interview?

"When do you think I might hear about the job?" I asked.

"Our department will contact you within ten days if you fit our current needs."

I wanted to ask what would happen if I did not fit their needs, but I figured I'd wandered far enough into none-of-my-business for one day.

Well, almost.

I did turn toward the lobby as I left his office, even though I was flattering myself if I thought the guy cared. Glass doors offered glimpses of temptation all along as I slow-walked the corridor. What excuse could I fabricate to sidle into one of those offices? How long could I peek through the glass without someone noticing?

A colorful map caught my eye through a closed glass door. For a moment, I thought it was a map of Barefoot Key. It was clearly blue gulf meeting sandy shore with lots of squares indicating properties.

I shifted my portfolio to my left arm and shoved through the door. No receptionist guarded the shiny white desk. At least I didn't think anyone was there.

Until a woman popped up from behind it. She eyed me with obvious disapproval. Maybe she wasn't alone behind that desk and resented my intrusion.

I looked at her scraped back hair, black-framed reading glasses, and buttoned up blouse. She was probably alone back there. My former savvy self would have admired her bookish all-business look, but I was starting to turn south these days with open-toed shoes, a suntan, and a closet filled with colorful tank tops.

"Where have you been?" she demanded. "Sunny Dreams said they'd send you right down and that was an hour ago."

I knew that name. It was the real estate company that swept through Barefoot Key two years ago. This must be how jailbirds feel when someone voluntarily opens the cage. I stood straighter and must have succeeded at impersonating the wayward courier from Sunny Dreams Real Estate above.

"Complications," I explained. Everyone has complications; it's a universal excuse and no one ever wants to hear what the complications are. It's usually too complicated.

The older woman handed me an oversized folder and a long poster tube. I guess whatever was in those packages was too large to email. With only a second's hesitation, I took the items. It's not stealing when you dress the part and someone hands you the goods.

"Thanks," I said. "Better get back right away."

I shoved the glass door open with my butt, backed into the hallway, and aimed for the lobby. It was a safe choice because the elevators were there and the pop-up secretary would assume I was getting on one to head skyward with my packages. It was also a safe choice because the glass doors to the parking lot were my intended target and my ticket to freedom.

I congratulated myself on two things as I counted my steps across the lot to my SUV. I was not running like a startled rabbit. And I was exercising restraint by not looking at what I held in my hands. No way was I snooping in the folder and tube until I got at least five miles away. Or at least one mile. Curiosity is stronger than restraint.

I tossed the documents on the floor of the back seat and made a safe getaway, stopping to look both ways before pulling out into Tampa traffic. I'd lived dangerously enough for one day already. And for what? For all I knew, my booty was an architectural drawing for a new helipad at corporate headquarters.

I pulled my ancient Chevy Tahoe into a fast food parking lot, cut the engine, and climbed into the backseat.

I remoted the doors locked and hunkered down behind tinted windows to pry privately into somebody else's business. The guilty feeling tightening the skin on the back of my neck was only partially caused by intercepting a courier package clearly not meant for me. I also felt bad about using the fast food restaurant's parking lot without buying something. It's the law of travel and commerce: if you use the restroom at a fast food joint, you have to at least get a small fry and a drink. Maybe a milkshake. The same rule probably applies to using their parking lots.

Was that smell fresh French fries? Hot from the fryer or not, I had sleuthing to do. Folder first. Easier to open.

It was a dud. A bunch of real estate contract summaries and listing statistics, none of them in Barefoot. All from some Florida town I'd never heard of.

Maybe the poster tube would pay off. I popped off one end of the cardboard cylinder and pried out the tightly rolled paper an inch at a time. Maybe it was nerves or maybe it was the battle of the tube, but sweat started to dampen my hair roots and make me wish I'd been smart enough to leave the car running, air conditioning on.

Triumphant, I finally extracted the poster and rolled it across my lap. What I found confirmed my belief in luck. Am I savvy? Sure. But falling into good fortune takes brains and effort to a higher mathematical power.

The map of Barefoot Key was colorful, accurate, detailed, and damning. Properties all over town, mostly concentrated in small groups, were outlined in red boxes. The most chilling aspect of the drawing was that the boxes were all named. I recognized the names, especially The Gull Motel.

If those red lines were drawn around people, the map would resemble a hit list.

And a hit list was exactly what I had spread out in my lap.

French fries and fast food etiquette would have to wait. I climbed over the seat, zipped on my seatbelt, and hauled ass out of the parking lot.

Chapter Fifteen

I called Rita on the way back to Barefoot and asked her to have Maria and LeeAnn stay over after their cleaning shifts ended. Despite her questions, I didn't reveal any details of my mission. Too paranoid from my theft and escape, I was afraid to risk the cellular airwaves. This was a topic for closed-door discussion with people I trusted. With way more combined experience in town than I could muster, my three Gull employees and colleagues would have insight on the map. Partly because his place was on the map—as well as the marina housing his father's fishing charter—I asked Rita to round up Skip for my bombshell meeting. Even if he didn't have insight, he made my hormones race and it might stimulate my thinking.

Convinced I was a knight in shining armor geared up to save Barefoot, I plotted all the way up the coastal highway about what I could do with my booty of information. Call a meeting of the Chamber of Commerce and warn them all they're on Sandshore's radar? A conspiracy theorist would kill for ammo like this.

When I parked in front of The Gull's office, I scooped up the poster and folder and marched into the lobby.

"We're going next door," Rita announced, not even saying hello first. "Skip's got his tool belt on too tight and he's all wound up for his grand opening tomorrow night. Says he doesn't have time to come over here, so we're going over there. LeeAnn and Maria are already there, probably half inebriated already."

I hesitated, feeling protective of the Gull. "We can't just lock the door and leave, can we?"

"That's what this is for." Rita held up a plastic sign with a suction cup on the back. The sign had a clock superimposed over a big yellow sun. It said *Back in ten minutes.*

"This will take longer than that," I said. Despite the cool air from the lobby air conditioning, a drop of sweat rolled off the end of my nose.

"Pull yourself together," Rita said. She pulled out a black marker, crossed off "ten minutes" and wrote in her cell phone number.

"Happy?" she asked.

"Better."

"You must have had one hell of an interview," Rita observed. "They offer you the CEO job?"

"Wouldn't want it. Wait until you see what's in here," I said, waving my poster roll.

Rita stuck the sign on the door at the same time a man's face appeared suddenly in the glass. I sighed and added a little groan for effect.

"I don't have time for him today," I said.

One hand on the door lock, Rita angled toward me and whispered, "Want me to get rid of him?"

It was Dalton from the FRTA. He'd been threatening a return visit, but I'd stalled him off. Not sure what direction anything was going around here, I had begun to regret involving him and his magazine.

"At least have him come back later," I whispered to Rita.

She opened the door a crack. "Nice to see you," she said. She used the voice she saved for difficult customers. They didn't know it, but she was picturing them covered in honey and ants when she spoke so sweetly.

Dalton had a laptop bag slung across his portly body, messenger style. He breathed heavily like he'd been hurrying all day long. He patted the bag and pushed one foot into the door opening. "I've got proofs," he said.

Because my mind was on the information in my stolen paperwork, for a moment I thought he was talking about proof of a whole other kind.

Rita held her ground, testing Dalton's resolve to get in the door. "We were just closing the office for a business meeting," she said. "Why don't you go downtown and get something to eat and we'll be glad to see whatever you've got in your bag later."

Without awaiting his answer, Rita shut the door, locked it, gave him a little wave. She grabbed my arm and her bulging ring of keys and shoved me through the back door toward the pool, locking the office slider behind her.

"He probably wanted to show us the final version of his magazine article," I said, finally figuring out what he wanted.

"Huh," Rita said, not slowing down. "Bet it's all pictures of you. The man's got a hard-on with your name on it."

Even in the heat radiating from the concrete pool patio, a full-body chill nearly knocked me down.

"I think he just needs attention," I said.

I had left the folder with the real estate listings on the office counter. I didn't think it offered much information and definitely no drama. Not like the rolled-up poster I clutched in my hand. When Rita and I strode through Skip's back door, Rita's perception and human understanding was instantly obvious. Skip was on a ladder hammering up colorful beer ads like he didn't care about the nail's feelings. As for LeeAnn and Maria, and as predicted by Rita, they had an empty pitcher between them and a full one waiting.

My big news would have to shout for attention. I elbowed between the two maids and spread the laminated map across their high-top table.

"Pretty," LeeAnn observed.

Maria giggled. Skip stayed on the ladder, only pausing in his hammering to give me a once-over. I still wore my ass-hugging navy blue pencil skirt, but my white blouse came untucked about fifty miles ago. Skip's once-over turned into twice. Maybe he liked the disheveled businesswoman look. Maybe he hoped he'd figure out why the hell I'd gone to Tampa if he looked hard enough.

"Crooked," LeeAnn yelled up at him. "Gotta go up with the left side."

"You're hammered," he muttered.

Divided loyalty gnawed me for a minute, but aesthetics won out. "She's right," I said. "Left side up an inch ought to do it."

Skip eyed the three of us and scratched the three-days of beard on his cheeks. He turned his attention to his beer banner and shoved one side up an inch. He gave me a look that asked a question.

"Better," I said. "Just right."

"With help like this, I should be open by next summer," he grumbled.

Actually, the big grand opening scheduled for tomorrow night was only a few days before Halloween. A costume party theme didn't take a lot of imagination as an idea. Add alcohol to the mix of costumes and loud music, and it's a party.

I only had one problem. No costume, no idea what to wear. During college, if someone said costume party, I'd retreated to the library and held my line behind bookshelves and a laptop screen. I guess I was a master of disguise since no one ever found me there.

I checked out Skip's ass on the ladder and wondered what he would wear to the party. The mood he appeared to be in, I thought he should go as Blackbeard the Pirate. But he'd already made it clear he was trying to get rid of the pirate motif left behind by Harvey. Maybe I should tell him modern pirates are sexy. Blame it on the movies.

"What are we supposed to be looking at here?" Rita asked. She knew I was looking at Skip's backside.

"On the poster," she added.

I forced my head back in the game. "It's Barefoot Key." I spread my arms, palms up, suggesting the answer was obvious.

"What about Barefoot?" Skip hooked an elbow on a ladder rung and stared down at us like we were toddlers messing up his clean house.

"Come see for yourself," I said.

I heard his complaint roll out on a sigh as he backed down the ladder.

Rita lightened the fresh pitcher by a glassful while we waited for Skip.

"See?" I asked.

Skip spread his hands across and leaned over the poster like a construction guy leans over a blueprint.

"So it's Barefoot," he said.

"And all the businesses have a red box around them," I said. Even to myself, I sounded like a kid explaining that there really was a big scary monster in her closet.

"Red boxes," I repeated, my righteous indignation fading at the dearth of enthusiasm from my supposed army.

"Not all of them," Rita said.

Everyone looked at the map. LeeAnn sloshed a drop of beer on it and used her elbow to swipe off the laminated surface.

"I see that now," Skip said, his tone implying interest for the first time.

"The Gull has a box," Maria said. "This bar does, too."

I considered asking Maria if she'd had any visions involving red boxes dooming Barefoot Key to the dumpster, but I didn't know what the effect of booze on visions was.

"Parts of downtown are boxed," LeeAnn said.

My business matrix brain hit overdrive as I looked for an answer, a logical pattern.

"All in groups," Maria said.

We leaned in like pirates elbowing each other to get at a treasure map. The red squares were all next to another one, none of them standing alone.

"What do all the groups have in common?" I said aloud.

Everyone looked perplexed. Silence. A faucet dripped behind the bar. Rita poured a glass of beer and handed it to me. We all took a swig.

Except Skip.

He shoved a hand through his hair and gazed around his not-ready-to-open bar with the crazed look wives get when their mother-in-law threatens to pop in.

"Maybe they're all in the toilet," he said. "Like me."

"Gull's not in the shitter," Rita said. She sat next to Maria, hip shoving her over. Centered over the poster, Rita put her elbows on both sides, owning it. "Know what I think?" she asked.

For the record, despite daily immersion and my generally savvy reputation, I was no good at reading Rita's thoughts. Probably safer that way, but sure as hell not as much fun.

"This came from the real estate company that's nosing around, right?" she asked.

I nodded.

"Not the same one that got their asses in a sling a few years back and lost money on this town. Is it?"

That question nagged me, too. Did the two companies have any connection? I'd think Sunny Dreams Real Estate would warn off Sandshore Realty, would tell tales of write-offs and losses. Maybe Sunny Dreams was hoping to thin the herd of real estate companies by watching a competitor fail.

"Not that I know of. Not officially anyway. But they seem to have offices in the same building."

"I'll drink to that," LeeAnn said.

We all looked at her. Her glass was empty again.

"What?" she asked. "It's a pretty poster. And we got a box. I feel sorry for all those places that didn't even get a mention."

"I'm driving you home," I said. My dramatic announcement and revelation was a rock at the bottom of a pond. My employees were drunk. And my pseudo-boyfriend looked like he wanted to make us all walk the plank.

Rita rolled up the map and handed it to me. "I'll call her a cab," she said. She glanced at Maria. "I'll call one for both of them."

She ushered them out the door with the most direct access to The Gull and closed it behind her. The click was loud in the empty bar. Skip and I faced off over the empty table.

"Why did you go to that stupid interview?" he asked.

I tightened the roll in my hand. "Curiosity," I said. Honestly, that's the reason I do most things. It takes a lot of self control not to knock on all the motel doors and ask people what they're doing in there.

"Satisfied?"

"Worse," I said. "There's something going on around here and I'm going to figure it out."

"Better figure out a way to keep that access road open or we're two islands in the stream."

"I know."

"Have you mentioned any of this to your aunt and uncle?" Skip asked.

I shook my head.

He gave me the look cops give shoplifting teenagers.

"I know," I said again. "But they're busy. Dealing with my headstrong and possibly crazy great aunt has kept them busy almost two months."

"They're not in much hurry to get back," he observed.

"Busy," I reiterated, waving my poster like a wand. "It's not easy to settle up someone's property and court dates before you park her in a rest home."

"I guess."

Skip dropped into a chair and pulled me into his lap. He kissed my neck right behind my ear and I forgot why I was here. I dropped the poster and let it roll under the table.

"Coming to my party?" he asked.

"I didn't get a formal invitation."

He used two fingers to turn my face and kissed me on the lips until I was a puddle of need, desire, and questions that could all be answered yes.

"You're invited," he murmured as he moved on to kissing my neck.

I wanted to go to the party. Desperately. In addition to having friends all over Barefoot and feeling like I belonged in this sleepy gulf coast town, I would take any opportunity to be within arm's length of Skip. Especially when thinking about my aunt and uncle told me my days here were probably numbered. As the days got shorter and the end of year started to get closer, I felt the pull of the job I thought I'd always wanted. A thousand miles away. These days, the pull was losing some of its grip.

"I have nothing to wear," I said.

"Come naked."

"To a costume party?"

"You'd win the contest," he said.

"There's a contest?"

"Always is. That's the fun of a costume party. Competition, fueled by alcohol, is the American Way. If you don't believe me, watch cable TV."

I faced Skip, our noses just touching. His eyes were warm caramels. Soft. Sweet. Irresistible.

"I've never been to an official costume party," I confessed.

Now the eyes were caramel surprise.

"We'll fix that. I've already planned our costumes."

"Our?"

"We're a pair. A matched set."

"Of what?" I blurted. Sure I wanted to know what our costumes were, but I also wondered how deep I should go diving for the meaning of *pair* and *set*. A more foolish romantic might consider that an offer or proclamation of some kind. When it came to Skip, I'd proven myself capable in the foolish department and hung my savvy reputation out to dry. Maybe it was his abs, his eyes, his impressive ability with his hands. Could be the tool belt. Hell, I wasn't fooling even myself. It was everything about him.

"I think I'll surprise you," he said. "I've never seen this look on your face in the six years I've known you. I think I've got you intrigued and I want to make it last. At least another day."

I wanted to protest, but my hormones were still fighting each other for supremacy in staged battles all over my body. And Skip knew it.

"I'll send over your costume tomorrow, just in time for the party."

"What if I don't like it? Or it doesn't fit?"

"Trust me," he said.

Chapter Sixteen

Although my brain was used to handling complex thought processes, I wasn't sure being savvy would help me figure out a poster with mysterious red boxes *and* how to handle a man like Skip McComber. Especially when that man seemed pretty confident about being able to handle me.

"Skip brought over a box about an hour ago," Rita told me when I got back from a Costco run. I carried bags of Halloween candy I'd bought in ridiculous quantities, but hey, it was bulk pricing. It had to be good, right? The Gull, like other businesses in Barefoot Key, would participate in the annual Halloween Walk. Kids in costumes paraded down the strip and harvested treats from every gift shop, restaurant, tourist trap, and motel. It was quite a haul for kids, good public relations for local commerce.

I dumped my bags on the check-in counter. "Almost afraid to ask," I said. Letting Skip pick out my costume for the party was one of the most personal things

I'd let him do. Aside from sex. That was personal, but there were hormones involved so it shaved off the responsibility of rational thought. Costumes are premeditated. They say a lot about a person.

"He looked happy," Rita said. "Like a kid getting away with something."

"Getting away with stealing cookies from the kitchen jar or getting away with stealing Grandma's prescription drugs and fencing them on the street?"

Rita looked thoughtful for five seconds. "Somewhere in between."

"Great."

"It's on your desk. I would've peeked, but the box is taped shut."

"And that stopped you?"

Rita shrugged. "This time."

I tore open a bag of Butterfingers and ate one, hoping the buttery sugary sweetness would get me in the Halloween spirit. "I'm going to do some paperwork and then I'll try it on. Whatever it is."

I retreated to my Uncle Mike's office—mine until they came back, whenever that was going to be—and shoved things around his big desk for a few minutes. Fact is, there was no paperwork I had to do right then. Rita had the reservation system under control. I had paid all the monthly bills. Payroll, small though it was, was complete. I'd even reorganized Uncle Mike's filing system and he'd be birthday-boy happy when tax season rolled around and he was already prepared for a sit-down with the tax preparer.

The expandable cardboard folder with the real estate papers I'd swiped from the Tampa office took up space on the edge of my desk mat. A quick glance in the backseat of my SUV yesterday told me there was nothing overtly incriminating in it. It was the poster with the red boxes around the livelihoods of people I knew and liked that grabbed my attention.

I looked at the big cardboard box that said "Savvy" on top in red magic marker. I had to face it. I slid open a drawer and grabbed a pair of scissors. I heard Rita on the phone in the outer lobby helping someone make a reservation. It was just me and the box. Palms sweaty, I clutched the scissors and cut the tape. The first thing I saw was sequins. Sparkles. Colorful, ethereal fabric. Was I a princess? A ballerina? I'll admit, I got my hopes up. I pulled the costume from the box and held it up.

Mermaid.

Holy shit.

Strapless, shaped boob cups, form-fitting. It was a mix of turquoise blue and sea green and glittered even in the afternoon light of the dingy office. A closet door in the office had a full-length mirror tacked to the inside of it. I swung the door open and held the costume in front of me. Maybe I hoped for magic.

The length was right, just above my feet in front. Although it was hard to tell because this costume had a long tail that would drag behind me far enough to qualify as an occupational hazard. It looked like it was made for someone skinnier than I am, but that was also hard to tell considering the fabric appeared to be some shimmery stretchy concoction.

There was only one way to know how bad this was going to look. I had to try it on. Perhaps I would discover that I was a drop-dead sexy mermaid and I'd never want to take it off. There was also the possibility that I'd be running to the drugstore for a Nixon mask and stealing my Uncle Mike's funeral suit from his closet.

I closed the office door, getting a quizzical glance from Rita. She'd probably give me five minutes before she breached the door to see me in my costume. I adjusted the ancient window blinds so no one could see in. And then I took off my clothes and shimmied into the mermaid costume.

Somewhere between adjusting the boob cups and tucking my ass into the costume, I realized I was going to need help. A zipper ran from my shoulder blades to my booty and the material wouldn't allow for error—one fatal catch of shimmery silk in the zipper and it would be belly up for the mermaid.

"Rita?" I called, opening the office door a sliver of an inch. Thank goodness the lobby was empty. I was more exposed than a lighthouse on a rocky island. "A little help?"

Rita shoved the door open and looked at me, half squeezed into a glittery mermaid mess of a costume. She laughed. "I love Skip."

The thought of Skip choosing this costume for me and bothering to order and deliver it gave my stomach a lurch, like how a fish feels when it's being reeled in beyond its control.

"I wonder what he's wearing?" Rita asked.

"He said our costumes matched."

She choked on a laugh. "He sure as hell isn't a manmaid, so I'm guessing maybe a sailor. Fisherman. Pirate. Something like that."

"Can you just come in here and zip this damn thing up?"

"Hell yes. I'd pay money to see you in it. But we may have to stuff those cups."

Rita locked the office door and squeezed and arranged me in the costume, flouncing my glittering tail out behind me like I was a bride and she was my maid of honor. She clucked her tongue, her face pure amusement.

"How's a savvy girl like you end up in a costume like this?"

"I think this is what my mother was talking about when she warned me about boys."

"I doubt it," Rita said. "She probably never saw this coming." She fished her cell phone out of her bra and snapped a picture. "I'll send this to your aunt and uncle. Might make the family Christmas card."

I grabbed for her phone, my scales and train knocking me off-balance so I swished over the corner of the desk. The file folder from the real estate company flopped onto the floor, spilling its contents like an ocean wave over the old tile.

"Geez," Rita said. "Don't get your tail in a twist. I was just kidding about the Christmas card."

I tried to bend over and pick up the papers, but Rita had the wardrobe advantage. Shorts and flip-flops never looked so good. How was I supposed to party in a costume like this? Maybe Skip didn't intend to dance with me and this was his way of gracefully getting out of it. I hoped he didn't intend to put me on display like a hooked fish. That would take a sizable amount of alcohol.

Rita scooped and shuffled the papers into a pile. There had to be dozens of real estate listings in the landslide on the floor. She straightened and looked at the stack in her hand.

"Nice houses for sale. Million-dollar stuff." She pulled out another paper from the stack. "This one's got a pool and a guest house. And I think the guest house has its own pool. Who the hell lives like that?"

"Nobody I know," I grumbled. My sequins itched my underarms and I was considering feigning illness to escape the party. If Rita thought I looked ridiculous, I didn't stand a chance.

She handed me another paper from the pile. This multi-million dollar estate had six fireplaces, a home theater, and a giant fence all around the property. My eyes dipped to the small picture of the realtor at the bottom with his contact information. Like I'd be calling to set up a tour.

The picture stopped me in my mermaid tracks. I maneuvered one butt cheek onto the desk corner, fighting for understanding.

"What?" Rita asked.

I held out the listing, my finger pointing to the small picture. "Does he look familiar?"

Rita took the paper over to the window and flipped the blinds open. "Shit," she said. "Looks a lot like that dumbass Dalton Longfellow."

"But that's not the name on there," I said.

"Dale Long," Rita read from the paper. "Close. Maybe they're cousins or something."

Maybe it was the blinds opening or good juices flowing from the tight squeeze in my costume, but ideas starting hitting me like a swarm of moths fighting over a street light.

"Wait a minute." I stood, swishing my tail behind me, righteous in my shimmering costume. "I think Dale Long and Dalton Longfellow might be the same person."

"That costume is messing with your head. I don't think a college nerd like you can handle all that cleavage and sparkle."

"I'm serious. Look at the picture. And those names? Come on. They're practically the same."

Rita considered my idea, looking alternately at me and the paper. "So what if they are? How come dorky Dalton is a slick real estate agent on the side? Hell, I figured he lived with his mother and bagged groceries on the weekends."

"What if his supposed articles—which we haven't seen—are just a front, a way for him to nose around Barefoot?"

"Did you sleep last night? Or did you stay up all night thinking of conspiracy theories? I better take that poster with the red boxes away or you're going to drift out to sea."

"It's not a conspiracy theory. Don't you see? There's something going on around here. And it's not good."

Rita's brow wrinkled. I think I was getting through to her.

"Want me to call another meeting of the drunks and pirates?" she asked.

"It's our only choice."

Rita went out to the lobby, shouted down the open corridor for LeeAnn and Maria, and used the landline to call Skip. I paced back and forth in the office, my tail swishing behind me like it was trying to clean up a big mess.

"What the hell happened to you?" LeeAnn asked. She was the first one through the door. I'd almost forgotten the multiple layers of stretchy shimmery fabric encasing my body as I wore a path around my uncle's office. At least I wasn't the only one in costume. Clearly, LeeAnn and Maria had been using an empty room to get dressed for tonight's party. I had already suggested they plan to stay over in an empty room so they could drink as recklessly as they wanted. Drinking recklessly was the only way I'd survive as a mermaid.

LeeAnn wore a cowgirl ensemble complete with killer boots and a rope. Maria was a gypsy fortune-teller, her dark wig spilling over her shoulders, a long swirly skirt nearly touching her toes. They looked almost as silly as I did, but I gave myself bonus points for showing more skin. And having a train.

Maria giggled. "I had a dream about you, but you were a fish, not a mermaid," she said.

Great. According to the psychic, I was meant to be a fish. I guess a mermaid is half-fish, so maybe Maria's dreams aren't so crazy. With my luck, Skip's costume would be a fisherman. Not a big stretch for a man whose family owned a fishing charter service.

"Skip's on his way. Didn't sound too happy about it, but he's coming," Rita said. "Think it's bad luck for him to see you in your costume before the party?"

"We're not getting married," I said. "It's a Halloween party in a bar."

"Too bad that's not white," LeeAnn said, "it would make a hell of a wedding gown with all that sparkly shit." She grinned. "Assuming you'd wear white."

Maria giggled again, and I was afraid to ask what kind of dream she might have had about that.

We froze when we heard the sliding patio door open and snap shut. It had to be Skip, but we—at least I—felt weird even talking about Skip and marriage in the same sentence. Two seconds later, he stood in the office door, filling it with his height, shoulders, and frustration. We all stared. Skip was the sexiest pirate—outside of movies—I'd ever seen. Bare-chested, low-slung knee-length breeches, boots. The most outrageously sexy part of his costume was the sword dangling from a red sash around his waist. Maybe it was Freudian, but somehow a sword looked just right on Skip. He had a red bandana tied over his head and an eye patch on a string dangling around his neck. I figured it was probably hard walking around with one eye and getting the bar ready. He could put the patch in place when the party got swinging. I knew he was in party-planning mode and his scowl suggested he didn't have time for my conspiracy theories.

The scowl, however, evaporated in an instant when he laid eyes on me. How could you see me in this ridiculous costume and not laugh? I could keep my mouth shut all night and still be the life of the party. A smile spread across his face and his eyes took three long passes of my mermaid self.

"Can you spin around?" he asked. He leaned one shoulder against the door frame. "I'd sure like to see the back view."

"Look at these," I said, ignoring Skip's question. I handed copies of the real estate flyers around and waited for a big reaction.

Maria whistled. "I like this house. It has a whole separate wing for the children. Maybe I could sleep at night. I wonder if it comes with a room over the garage for my husband?"

"See this one?" LeeAnn said. "Gourmet kitchen takes up half the main floor. I could make fish tacos that would make Charlie Tuna weep if I had a kitchen like that."

"I think you're missing the point," I said.

Skip stared at his flyer. "Mine's for a gas station and convenience store. Not as fancy as all yours, but it's on a corner. Can't beat the location."

Rita huffed out a breath. "Look at the picture at the bottom. The realtor."

There was a beat of silence while they all looked.

"Never heard of Dale Long, but this guy sure looks like that stupid reporter from the old farts magazine who's been hanging around," Skip said.

"He *is* that guy," I insisted.

Maria and LeeAnn took a closer look. LeeAnn got her reading glasses out of the front pocket of her checkered cowgirl shirt.

"Just as ugly," she said.

"I had a bad feeling about that guy," Maria said, shaking her head and looking sinister. With her dark looks and costume, she could scare people—at least children—with her gypsy gig. "He's leading a double life. Probably cheating on his wife, too."

I tried to picture Dalton or Dale or whatever his name was with a wife. I shrugged. "I haven't figured the whole thing out, but we're going to. Here's what I know. The real estate company that bought a bunch of properties a few years ago is affiliated with the company that's shopping around right now. They have offices in the same building. I saw it for myself when I went to that bogus interview."

"So they're both throwing away money in Barefoot," Skip said. His eyes wandered to the door, probably hoping for an escape route back to his party setup.

"Businesses, especially huge ones that would have these properties for sale," I pointed to the flyers for emphasis, "don't throw money away. They throw money at stuff. I had thought they were looking for tax write-offs. Buying properties and then devaluing them in a later sale. But that doesn't explain the whole picture. Or the map."

I grabbed the map from the top of the filing cabinet and spread it over my uncle's desk. "They're systematic. They buy properties, marked with red boxes, and then maybe they plan to get the neighboring ones, also marked with boxes."

"So they lose twice the money," Rita said.

"So they gain twice the control," I said. "They're playing a game. If you devalue property, you breed desperation. People who would not normally sell will sell if they're afraid everything's going down. Like Jeanette."

I had them with Jeanette. No one ever imagined the owner of Sunshine Souvenirs next door selling out. Especially when it put both The Gull and Skip's bar out of driving access and in big trouble. Had Jeanette been coerced to sell? Maybe. Or maybe it was just like she said, someone made her a decent offer and she grabbed it before property values plummeted any more in Barefoot Key.

"So," LeeAnn said, her reading glasses giving her a professorial look I envied, "these real estate companies work together to buy up, crap on, and then re-buy properties in an effort to sink values all over town."

"Yes," I said, feeling like a piece of the puzzle was just out of reach.

"Why?" Maria said. "Sounds like someone hates our sleepy little town."

"Or loves it," Skip and I said at the same time, a stereo revelation in the quiet office. Our eyes met, a strange understanding gleaming in both of them.

I leaned over the map, my mermaid cleavage practically spilling over and revealing the toilet paper Rita had stuffed in there. Skip leaned over the other side of the desk and made an obvious reconnaissance mission down the front of my costume.

"Save it for later," I whispered. Everyone heard it anyway. It was no surprise we were sleeping together. What no one, including us, knew was where it was leading. Given our costumes for the party, I thought there was a chance he'd kidnap me and have his way with me on the open seas. I'd be fine with that.

"If someone wanted to buy a bunch of contiguous parcels in this area, this is how they would do it," I said.

"A bunch of what?" Rita asked.

"Properties that are connected," I said. "Like they had big plans for the area, but needed a chunk of land."

"Sounds like it would take lots of planning and balls to pull something off like that," LeeAnn said.

"Businesses employ people who do nothing but long-range planning. As for balls, I'd say they'd need information more than anything."

"Like inside information?" Skip asked.

I nodded. "If something big is being planned for Barefoot, how come none of us know about it?"

Nobody answered.

"Seriously," I said. "You've all lived here forever, I've been to Chamber of Commerce meetings. No one seems to know anything."

"Wait a minute," Skip said. He fiddled with his sword. Maybe it helped him think. Or gave him confidence. "This is just gossip. Probably drunken gossip since I got it from my dad. And it's old news."

"What?" I asked.

"A few years ago, there was some talk about a new airport going in around here somewhere." He paused. "A big airport. International deal like Orlando and Miami."

I crossed my arms and wrinkled my brow. Maybe I looked like a savvy-thinker and maybe I just looked like an angry mermaid. This gossip didn't make much sense to me, but I wasn't exactly a local. The other women in the room were nodding like they knew something I didn't.

"Why does this area need another international airport?" I asked. "Isn't the Tampa airport just an hour away?"

"Uh-huh. But it can't grow," Skip said. "It's landlocked. There was talk of moving up the coast. Heard they were looking at a place about thirty more miles up, but it's some kind of protected wildlife area."

"So you think Barefoot is being targeted for a possible airport? That's why this company is trying to buy it all up?" I asked.

"Haven't heard anything lately about it," Skip said. "Guess we all thought the idea died out a few years back."

"Maybe it didn't," LeeAnn grumbled. "Maybe Barefoot Key isn't as worthless as it looks."

"Values could skyrocket," Rita said. "Somebody who owned a big enough chunk of ground could be sitting pretty."

Maria rolled out the desk chair behind me and plunked into it. I couldn't sit in my costume, so it was fair game.

"You all right?" Rita asked, her gaze on Maria behind me. I turned and saw her face. Strained. Pale.

"I had a dream like this," she said. "But it wasn't just an airport, there were huge ships—cruise ships all over Barefoot Key. Tourists lapping up ice cream, The Gull no longer the same." She put her head in her hands and rocked side to side. "The Gull had a continental breakfast and an indoor pool. Floors and floors of rooms. All that cleaning. Terrible."

"You and your visions," LeeAnn said, her tone teasing. "But maybe you're right this time."

"So what's the deal with dorky Dale or Dalton or whoever the heck he is?" I asked.

I rolled Maria aside and leaned over the computer on Uncle Mike's desk. I searched both names. Dalton Longfellow turned up pretty much zilch. An old man in California, the name of a porn star in New Jersey. Not our man. At least I hoped not. Dale Long also turned up some obviously false hits. A semi-pro ball player in Arizona, a private pilot in Maine, a watercolor artist in Alaska. And a member of the Florida state tourism board. I searched farther. Dale Long was a well-connected realtor who had friends in high places, including a brother-in-law in the Florida state senate. I was starting to think he also had friends in low places.

I shared the relevant results with my conspiracy club. "So dorkman Dalton isn't really a writer for a travel magazine?" Rita asked.

"I don't think so. Looks like that's his undercover job." I flounced around the desk, swirling my tail behind me as I went. I took another look at the map. "I think the real estate company sends Dalton out to supposedly ask questions for an article for a sham magazine, but he's really a snoop. Finds out who's got a solid business, who might be interested in selling, who's on the rocks."

"That little shit," Rita said.

"I had a bad feeling about him," Maria ventured.

LeeAnn rolled her eyes.

"So Dalton's a mole, and somebody's trying to swindle a load of property in town here which may or may not be for an airport and cruise line combination," Skip said. He sounded skeptical.

"I saw the ships," Maria insisted. "In my vision."

To my surprise, Skip nodded. "I believe you. Something's been nagging me for a while. Dad has mentioned it, but you know." He didn't have to finish the sentence. My companions all knew Jude McComber was a drunk with a reputation for running his mouth. He was a friendly drunk, not a mean one, but he'd been a principal disseminator of information in Barefoot Key for decades. And not all of it true. "Here's the thing. The guy who owns the marina where Dad docks his fishing boats has had offers. Good ones. For the whole bundle. He owns a lot more coastal footage than people realize."

"Do you think any of these offers are coming from Sandshore Realty?" I asked.

"Probably. But he's turned them all down. Got a sentimental attachment to the land. It was in his family. Last month, though, he changed the contracts for all the dockage. Used to be two-year contracts. He changed them to six months."

"And?"

"And now I wonder if he plans to bail out in six months. Maybe this time he got an offer he can't refuse," Skip said.

I took another hard look at the map, not even caring that a chunk of stuffing from my mermaid cups flopped out on the desk. The marina in question was outlined with a huge oblong box on the map. It had to be a half-mile of coastline. And it was surrounded by other red-boxed properties. In fact, a trail of properties, like a highway, led straight to the marina. The Gull was right on the path.

I pointed to the boxes and tried to look serious despite my ruffles. "That's your answer," I said. "Cruise line terminals there. A highway running right through here. A big international airport right out here on the edge of town where there's plenty of room and a new power station. What I can't imagine is how they think they can pull this off without anyone knowing what they're up to."

We all pondered that. LeeAnn and Maria fidgeted with their costumes. It was silent a moment.

"This is bullshit," Rita finally said. "Somebody downtown has to know something. I say we go ask'em."

Chapter Seventeen

Because she was the only one not encumbered by a ridiculous costume, Rita got elected to drive my old SUV the short distance across a bridge and into downtown Barefoot Key proper. The rest of us were piled in, our costumes unwieldy, itchy, and, in Skip's case, downright dangerous. We tossed his sword on the floor the second time he nearly took out Maria in her gypsy costume. None of us could risk bad karma right then.

The city offices were located in a building that looked too fancy for the name. It had been an ornate hotel in its early days over a hundred years ago when it seemed that the railroads would claim this edge of Florida. They didn't, but the building lived on, its stone columns and elegant windows sitting quietly under a tiled Spanish roof.

We barreled out of the SUV and headed for the city manager's office. No idea if and what he knew about these real estate rumors, not a care for how crazy we all looked.

Skip hooked an arm around me in the elevator and kissed my neck. "Arrgh," he said.

"I thought you were trying to lose the pirate motif with your new décor. Goodbye Harvey's Pirate Emporium, hello Skip's Beach Shack."

He shrugged. "If it's not broke, I guess it's one less thing I have to fix. Besides, pirates need a drink, too." He looked at me suggestively. "They have all kinds of terrible needs."

"You'll have to think about your needs later," LeeAnn said. The elevator doors pinged, opened, and dumped us all out on the third floor.

The expression on the face of the city manager's frontline receptionist suggested she hadn't expected a mermaid, pirate, gypsy, cowgirl, and one normal person. No one would. I vaguely recognized her, although I doubted I was recognizable in my mermaid getup.

"I remember you," Rita said. "You spent a week at The Gull a month or so ago. Thought you'd passed on through town."

She did look familiar and I recalled her quiet residency in room eighteen. Today, something about the

244

secretary looked dangerous. She gave Rita the wrinkled forehead and clenched jaw look an ex-wife gives the new mistress. I hoped she wasn't one of the thousands of Florida residents who'd taken to flea markets and self-defense seminars to pick up a concealed carry permit. We were living dangerously.

I could only take tiny little steps in my costume, so I speed-tiptoed to the counter and laid a fin on it. "We're here to talk to the city manager," I said.

She eyed her purse and I hoped she wasn't mentally reviewing how to use a .22 in self-defense. Mouth drawn in a straight line, she returned her attention to me. "Do you have an appointment?"

All my life, I've followed the rules. I've been the good girl, relying on brains and hard work when others cheated their way through school. Making complete stops at four-way intersections. Even when no one was looking. Never embellishing my charitable donations on my tax forms. But this was no time for demure civility.

"We don't need one. The city manager works for us," I said, gesturing at my band of costumed warriors. My business minor was finally worth something! I was confident about city finances. At least, confident enough for the situation. "Our tax money pays his salary, so I think he can take ten minutes and hear us out."

She dropped one shoulder, half-glancing over it at the door behind her. Her expression told me he was in there. The door was open a couple inches and we'd made no effort to be quiet. If he had nothing to hide and any mercy for his secretary, he'd be out here in a minute. We heard the murmur of voices, almost whispers, from the office.

"We could come back tomorrow," Skip said. I was about to flip him with my mermaid tail and berate him for trying to be nice and back down. But I didn't have to. "We can always ask someone else what they know about the land-buying scheme going on around here," he continued loudly, "maybe the newspaper can shed some light on it."

A chair scraped on tile and the office door opened wide. The city manager stood wildlife-still, a fight or flight expression fleeting across his face when he saw my costumed menagerie. Even in my state of righteous indignation, I found it in my heart to feel sorry for the guy for just a moment. I'd be nervous, too, facing a group like mine.

But we couldn't let him off the hook until we learned what we came to find out. Was Barefoot Key being parceled and sold out by someone on the inside? Anthony White had been heralded in the local paper for his many projects supposedly improving the quality of life around Barefoot Key. He'd rebuilt the highway ramp off the interstate in order to bring more tourist traffic into town. Cleaned up an old factory that was designated a brown field by the EPA so the property, a large parcel in the heart of Barefoot, could now be sold and developed. Found grant money to put in a new power station right inside the city limits so Barefoot Key could generate far more power than it could possibly use. Sure, the city could sell the power to other cities on the grid...but all these improvements could also signal a sale of a whole other kind.

"Are you here to take me to the party," he asked, a forced smile not fooling anybody. His smoker's skin and yellow teeth were not flattered by office fluorescent. He looked truly frightening.

"You were invited," Skip said. "The whole city was."

"Very nice what you've done with that bar," White said. "Too bad not everyone in this town sees the value of upgrading."

I swear he looked at me when he said it. Sure The Gull hadn't changed during my lifetime, but I wasn't going on the defensive. I was part of the offensive line in this mission.

"Do you know Dalton Longfellow?" I asked.

White cleared his throat and made a barely-noticeable glance at an unknown person in his office.

"Also known as Dale Long," I prompted. What the hell? In my opinion, the gloves were off. The scales had fallen from my mermaid eyes. I wanted to settle this.

White did not speak, but he looked at a spot behind his door and cocked his head as if he were asking a question. A chair creaked. And dumpy Dalton appeared. Strangely, he wasn't dumpy at all. He wore a polished suit and had his hair slicked back. I swear he looked thinner—maybe he wore one of those gut-sucking garments. Spanx for men. Either way, he was scarier this way. More imposing.

Skip held his eye patch between his fingers and snapped the elastic string, a strangely threatening gesture. "Maybe you can show us a copy of your article for the travel magazine," he said.

I thought this was a good opening, especially since Dalton had been nosing around ostensibly wanting to show me his writing. I'd turned him away yesterday, and now I wondered what would have happened if I'd heard him out.

No one said anything. Skip continued to snap his eye patch. The city manager and his guest eyed each other, both of them appearing to search for a way out.

"Or maybe you'd like to show us some nice real estate for sale," I said. I didn't want to let Skip have all the fun. I held up the folder of real estate flyers. Dalton's eyes fell on it and I had no doubt he recognized it.

White tried to reclaim his territory and right his ship. "It appears you've discovered that my friend here wears many hats. If that's all you have to say, we're all busy and I'm sure you could make an appointment to come back at a more convenient time."

LeeAnn unrolled the poster of Barefoot Key and held it in front of her, only the top of her cowgirl hat visible. Dalton and White looked at it and exchanged glances again.

"Where did you get that?" White demanded.

"From his corporate office," I said, pointing at Dalton.

"Stolen," Dalton said, his voice full of fake umbrage.

I crossed my arms and cocked my head. "Give me a break. It was handed to me accidentally. And that doesn't change what it reveals."

I really hoped I wasn't bluffing or full of inflated conspiratorial baloney. What if we really did imagine what we were afraid to see in all this evidence I had liberated from the real estate building?

White wasn't backing down. He leaned against the paneled wall separating his office from the reception area. "And what have you all conjured up in your imaginations? You barge in here and act like you've uncovered a great mystery. But what do you have?"

The secretary rolled her chair over, removing herself from the direct line between my group and the manager and his guest. Maybe she didn't think a minimum wage secretarial position was worth taking someone else's crap. She parked by a low counter and watched. I would have taken my lunch break if I were her.

"You know what I think?" Rita asked. "I think you and two-face here are in cahoots. I think you've been using him to pry into people's businesses in this town. He's been cuddling up to you so his big fancy company can buy up half of Barefoot for their plan."

LeeAnn lowered the map and laid it on the receptionist's counter. The secretary stood and tried to get a look at it. "Back off," Maria said, getting in the other woman's face and giving her a scary gypsy look.

"Just curious," the secretary said. She held up her hands in a gesture of neutral innocence. "Wondered what you've got there."

"Other than some lame suspicion. You've got nothing on me," White said.

"I wonder what people in Barefoot will say about that when this gets around," I said. "I think they won't want to hear that their city manager has been secretly working with a company that wants our town's property so bad it's willing to steal to get it."

"Are you accusing me of theft?" Dalton asked.

"I sure as hell am," I said. My sequins sparkled in the office lighting, bolstering my confidence. "Buying properties and then selling them back to the same company at a loss is fraud. Especially if that company takes a tax loss. I think it would be pretty interesting to have a look at your company's books."

"You really think we'd be that stupid?" Dalton asked.

"Please," I scoffed. "I could name five cases involving companies a lot smarter than yours that have swindled their way into a jail cell." This was true. Cautionary tales were all over Wall Street and cable news. "Our next phone call is going to be to the police."

Dalton and White exchanged a look and went on the offense, catching us all off-guard because none of us expected them to get physical. White lunged for the folder in my hand at the same time Dalton lunged for the rolled-out poster. Skip grabbed White just before he got my folder. My costume made it tough for me to react, but pirate garb was made for adventure. Skip swashbuckled the city manager right to the ground.

Unfortunately, Dalton was too quick for Cowgirl LeeAnn. He nearly got the poster, swiping it from the counter a half second before she grabbed for it. Dalton spun around, poster clutched in his hands, and tried to maneuver his big body past the secretary.

To everyone's surprise, the secretary did not retreat. "Freeze!" she said. We all cut our eyes to her. She held a gun trained on Dalton. "You're under arrest." She spared a quick glance at White, writhing on the ground under Skip. "You, too. If I had to work for you one more day, I was probably going to shoot you just for fun."

"Who are you?" I asked, stupefied.

"Undercover agent, IRS," she said. "We've been after these swindlers for years. Hard to catch them at their own office. They're crafty. So we branched out and followed the money."

"I want a lawyer," Dalton said, still being held at gunpoint by the secretary.

"You'll get your chance. This guy," she said, pointing at White, "has made a nice little profit off real estate speculation."

Skip ground the heel of his pirate boot a little deeper into the soft flesh of White's shoulder.

"Change is coming," White grunted. "Backward Key can't stay this way forever."

"Hey," Maria said, giving White an evil eye. "Watch your mouth." She leaned close and whispered something none of the rest of us heard. White turned three shades paler and stopped resisting Skip's restraining foot.

"See if you can get me a few officers from the police station downstairs," the agent said, "and we'll put these guys away while we finish off our case."

After the schemers were hauled downstairs by some local police officers, I asked Maria what she said to White.

"I told him about a dream I had involving him," she said.

"It must have been some dream, judging from his reaction."

"You don't want to know," she said.

I decided I was glad Maria was on my side.

"Party time," Skip said. "You driving, Rita?"

"I'll drop all you clowns off and then go home and get in costume," she said. "You'll never guess what I'm wearing."

After the events of the past few hours, I was afraid to ask.

Chapter Eighteen

It was the calm before the storm. The lights were still full power, the kegs were loaded, the chairs neatly shouldered up to high-tops and tables. In about ten minutes, Skip would throw open the doors to customers for the first time since he'd sunk his savings and future in the former Harvey's Pirate Emporium. Now Skip's Beach Shack, it still felt like pirates could swagger through the door and raise some hell. Maybe the owner's costume was no accident.

The sight of Dalton and the city manager being hauled downstairs by Barefoot Key police officers was fresh in my mind, but unanswered questions had taken over the stage.

"What now?" I asked Maria, LeeAnn, and Rita. We were the first patrons, but also acting as staff. We'd help out by checking IDs, pouring a few rounds, and judging the costume contest. We were already taking our jobs seriously, only sharing one pitcher so far.

"Now people in Barefoot are gonna get some justice," Rita said. Her costume mystified everyone on her initial arrival. Because we thought she was a tub of butter. When she pointed out the black letters clearly labeling her cardboard tub *Margarine*, LeeAnn was the first to put it together. *Marga-Rita*. A more clever play on words than I was expecting, but who could argue with a hooch-themed costume at a grand opening for a bar? I guess I wasn't the only savvy one around.

"Hard to pay the bills on justice," LeeAnn said. "People whose property is worth seagull-shit or already been sold aren't going to eat justice for dinner. What happens to those places?"

I'd already thought about what would happen to properties like the Sunshine Souvenir Stand next door and many others just like it. Sure, the criminal masterminds at the real estate company might do time over their fraud and wouldn't be getting their hands on any more of the red boxes on their poster, but what about the properties they'd already bought?

"Public auctions," I said. "Sheriff sales, something like that."

We sat around a table in front of the bar. Long faces and empty glasses.

"What if someone had some capital?" Maria asked. "What could a pile of money do to help in this case?"

I thought about that for a minute. "Hypothetically speaking, someone could buy the properties near fair market value and help restore the balance around here. Could also finance current owners, maybe help them stay afloat in their mortgage and location."

Maria nodded vigorously, looking like a gypsy who was just offered an audience with the Queen to direct national affairs.

"But it would take a *huge* pile of cash. A hundred thousand here, eighty thousand there, plenty in the bank for reserves and collateral." I shook my head. "Even if we knew anyone who had access to cash like that, how would we convince someone to take a chance on Barefoot Key? Especially since the airport and cruise line terminal thing is probably bust now."

Maria set a crystal ball on the table in front of her. If it was a costume prop, it was a damn realistic one. She stroked it dramatically. Skip left his bar-polishing job and came over, standing at a corner of the table occupied by the four of us.

"I'm seeing a group of women in Barefoot Key," Maria said. "Good Catholic women."

I wasn't sure where the Catholic Church was on the subject of gypsies, but everyone likes to be labeled good.

"The women have a treasure. A big treasure," Maria continued.

I suddenly remembered Maria's admission to me about her internet gambling success and her insinuations that some of her church friends were possessed of the all-seeing eye as well. It was almost too much to hope for, but...

"The treasure can only be used to help others," Maria said, "or the source of knowledge might dry up."

"Jesus Christ," LeeAnn said. "Are you telling us your crazy-ass visions have actually amounted to something?"

Maria dropped her gypsy act and looked almost repentant. "It started small. A thousand, thirty thousand, a hundred thousand. We kept picking winners in the market. Bought low, got lucky, sold high."

"And you're telling us—" I began.

"Two million. And counting," Maria said. She shoved her words away from her body like they were an evil burden. "We've been meeting in secret, not knowing what to do with the money. None of us have told our husbands. They'd want to buy a boat or a motor home. Maybe start drinking."

I could sympathize with their priorities, but could also see Maria's point.

"Let me get this right," Rita said. "You church ladies have used some kind of vision to play the market—"

"And do some internet gambling," Maria added.

"Nice," Rita said, smiling. "And now you have a crapload of money you feel guilty about?"

Maria nodded.

"In the right hands," Skip said, "that amount of money could be used to rescue properties in immediate danger and create a fund to sustain future local development. Like a revolving loan fund for local businesses."

Maybe it was my mermaid costume combined with my share of the margarita pitcher, but I felt tingly all over.

"How would this work?" LeeAnn asked.

"You'd need someone, or a group of people like a board, to manage a fund like that," Skip said. "Would have to be someone the locals trusted, someone who's proven she cares about Barefoot Key."

He snapped on his eye patch and bored me with a one-eyed stare. Rita, LeeAnn, and Maria fixed me with their attention, too.

"I can't be in charge of your booty," I said. *They weren't serious, were they?*

"Why not?" Maria asked.

"I don't live here," I said.

"Huh," Rita grunted. "In an outfit like that, you sure look like you do. And how about your Barefoot Key t-shirts and that tacky tube top sundress? You can't wear those up north."

"So I have the wardrobe now, but come on. I finally got into the hotel management trainee program."

"You did?" Rita asked.

I nodded.

"You didn't mention that," Skip said.

No one looked impressed.

"It's a fancy hotel," I insisted.

Again, not impressing anyone.

"In Chicago," I finished. Even I wasn't buying what I was selling.

"I had a dream about you," Maria said. "You were on a beach. With three barefoot children."

"We're going to need another pitcher," I said.

****

The party had been raucous for at least an hour when a mysterious pair of gorillas showed up. Their black costumes were more anatomically correct than anyone—even drunkards—wanted to see. One was obviously male and the other female. The identities of the wearers were completely concealed under fake primate skin and fur.

Rita bumbled over in her big tub of margarine. "Who you think they are?" she asked.

The gorillas hovered near the door for a moment, their masked faces turned up and around like they were seeing the bar for the first time. Not a surprise since most of the hundred or so guests were also seeing the grand reveal of Skip's remodel.

"Think they're friendly?" I asked.

Rita scrunched her face, staring and evaluating. "Hard to tell with primates. Maybe I'll go nose around'em, see if I can figure it out."

"They could be federal agents or real estate agents or Hollywood talent scouts for all we know." I smoothed my mermaid ruffles. "It's been a hell of a day."

Rita scrutinized me and leaned as close as she could in her big costume. She shouted over the noise of the DJ and the bar. "You thinking about sticking around and handling the church ladies' guilt money?"

I shrugged, my boobs almost popping out of my sequined cups. "I think I better think about it. A lot depends on my aunt and uncle. If they ever come back from Michigan, I'd be interested in hearing their take on all this."

Rita looked around the room like she was thinking hard about something serious. "Can't ignore Maria's visions, I guess. Hell, I thought she was kind of a nut, but now—" she spread her arms wide, grinning broadly, "I can't tell the smart ones from the fools."

Rita moved on, bumping past clowns, bikers, priests, superheroes, princesses, and a farmer/devil pair with matching pitchforks. I didn't want to know if they were an intentional pair, but it sure looked that way.

I shifted onto an end bar stool, adjusted my costume, and parked my half-full glass on the shiny bar. Skip's handiwork was evident everywhere I looked. The pirate bar mixed tacky old motifs with a shinier beach vibe. Like Blackbeard had found his hipster side.

"Wonder who's in those suits," Skip said as he leaned toward me and pointed behind me at the mystery primates.

"No idea," I said, swiveling to look, "but they sure are having fun." The gorillas were performing all kinds of antics—scratching armpits while shaking their booties, knocking hats off people's heads, stealing drinks.

I began to suspect they were not federal agents when they rubbed their surprisingly realistic nipples together and got loud applause from the well-lubricated crowd.

"Something about the big one seems familiar," Skip observed.

Disturbing, but true. The gorillas bowed for the crowd and ambled over to the bar. The big gorilla held up two fingers and Skip obliged him by pulling two drafts and setting them on the bar. They were right next to me, but I doubted they could see very well out of the small eye-holes in their masks.

I turned toward them so they got a good view of my face, and I was immediately crushed in a vinyl and faux fur hug. I thought I might suffocate at first and wondered if being molested by two primates was an occupational hazard of costume parties.

And then it hit me.

"Aunt Carol?" I asked.

The smaller ape nodded enthusiastically.

"Uncle Mike?" I said.

The big ape did a little dance.

They were back! Like my half-woman, half-fish costume, I was also wavering between two states of being. Sure I was glad to see my favorite relatives, and their return must mean good news for Aunt Gwen. But I'd started to feel just right in flip flops. Comfortable showing some shoulder. Happy in my role as guardian of The Gull.

Maybe my extended vacation was over and it was time to get my wool coat out of storage and take up my post at the glossy Chicago hotel. *Damn.*

Mike and Carol pulled off their ape heads and picked up their drinks. We clinked glasses and toasted without even saying anything, just happy to see each other.

"We have a lot to tell you," Aunt Carol said. "And something important to ask, too."

"After the party," Uncle Mike added. "We've got to catch up, but I want to have fun. Can't believe what Skip's done with the old pirate emporium."

The party—aided and abetted by a kickass DJ and plentiful libations—made its official last call at two a.m. after which Maria and LeeAnn staggered back to The Gull where rooms waited. Rita's nephew Ralph—disproving the working theory about his general uselessness—arrived in time to drive her home. Other guests, in bedraggled costumes that didn't quite stand up to dancing, wandered off.

Only Skip and I were left. Alone. Mike and Carol, tired from their trip, made it to midnight and headed to their owner's suite at The Gull. If I'd known they were coming, I'd have aired out their apartment, musty from two months of emptiness. But I figured they'd be so happy to be home, maybe they wouldn't mind.

"We'll clean up tomorrow," Skip said, his dazed expression touching on every surface of his bar. He looked tired but happy. And he should be. Judging from the crowd, the money he'd sunk into the place on blind faith was going to pay off over time.

"No argument from me." I had my tail pinned up and my hair down. Emotionally, I was a seagull riding the waves. Up, down. Up, down. Going? Staying? I didn't know.

"If you were wondering where to go now that the party's over," Skip said. "I'm hoping you'll stay right here." He looked closely at me and put his bare arms around me.

If Skip ever gave up the bar, he could probably become a mind reader and join Maria's group of financial prophets.

Or maybe I was just easy to read.

"My bachelor pad is nicer than the walk-in cooler," he added, sweetening the deal.

"And there's no hurricane," I said.

"And you don't have to babysit The Gull tonight."

My fins drooped. "I'll miss The Gull."

"Not if you don't leave," he said.

I glanced around the bar. Skip was born in Barefoot Key. His family owned a local business. He would stay here probably forever, never considering going anywhere else.

And me? I could move to Chicago, toss on my suit and cater to strangers.

Or.

"I want you to stay," Skip said.

"Tonight?"

"For a start."

"And then?"

"Tell you what. Give me a chance to get you out of the mermaid costume, and you'll forget you ever thought about walking the plank."

"You're on, pirate."

****

When morning rolled around and I watched the sun slowly light the sea through the tiny window of Skip's bar-apartment, I'd made my decision. I stood naked at the window, not wanting to squeeze back into the mermaid costume, my only clothing available. I watched a gull swoop and land on the early morning gulf.

I heard a slight rustle and Skip wrapped his naked body all around me.

"I hope you're not plotting your escape route," he said, nuzzling my neck with his scratchy morning beard.

"I'd have to borrow a fishing boat from your dad's fleet. You could be my captain."

He shook his head.

"Okay, pirate if you prefer that title."

Skip sighed, his breath brushing my bare shoulder. "I should probably tell you something I've been hiding for almost all my life."

The gull took off, swooped low, and dropped a load of crap on a beach chair someone had left out on the sand.

I sucked in a breath. "Afraid to ask," I admitted.

"Because my dad took over his fishing charter from his dad, everyone always expected I would do the same."

I nodded. I'd wondered about that when I heard he bought the bar.

"But I can't," he continued.

"Is this because of your dad's drinking?"

"Nope." Stubble scraped my ear as he shook his head. "Fact is," he paused and I counted three full breaths. "I can't be a fisherman because… I get seasick."

I wanted to laugh with relief. Seasick? This was the big family secret?

"Really," he said, filling in my silence. "Major motion sickness. Hose-off-the-side-of-the-boat puking. Never-ending."

I turned into his arms and kissed him.

"Why are you telling me this now?"

"Because I want you to decide what you want. You don't have to do anything just because everyone always expected you to. Or because you're really savvy."

This was the sweetest thing Skip had said to me in the six years I'd known him. He didn't know that my decision was made already.

"I don't get seasick," I said.

He chuckled. "You have no idea how lucky you are."

With Skip naked and squeezed up against me, I actually did know I was very, very lucky.

"Maybe I'm crazy to give up the fancy-pants hotel opportunity in Chicago and move to Barefoot Key," I said. "But there are some pretty compelling reasons to stay here."

"Such as?" he asked, pulling me a little tighter.

"For one, I like the challenge of managing the Barefoot Key Revitalization Fund."

"And?"

"The wardrobe. I'm really getting used to bare toes and tank tops."

Skip kissed me on the lips like he owned me.

"Anything else?" he asked.

"You tell me," I teased.

"If you tried to leave, I'd put on my pirate costume and come after you."

"That's the best offer I've ever had."

Skip walked me over to his bed. "I can do even better than that."

****

That afternoon, showered and wearing fresh shorts and a tank top, I faced my aunt and uncle over a patio table. They looked nervous, but excited, a déjà vu to two months ago when they asked me to take over the Gull while they went home to take care of Carol's mother.

"How is Aunt Gwen?"

"We got the charges dropped," Aunt Carol said. "Again."

"This time," Uncle Mike added. "Afraid the neighboring vineyards might be less tolerant of her grape-stealing next time."

"Well," I said, going for a cheerful tone. I still had happy hormones from my morning with Skip beaming sunshine all over me. "At least the harvest is over for the year. How much trouble can she get into now?"

Carol rolled her eyes. "She had big plans for a holiday light display. Probably enough to either blow out power for the whole street or earn her a civil lawsuit."

Mike sat back in the aluminum patio chair and cast a wistful glance over the motel. LeeAnn rolled her cleaning cart along the upstairs corridor, rumbling over the concrete cracks. I figured she must be having a good morning because she smiled and waved cheerfully. On another morning, she would be just as likely to give us all the finger. In a nice way, of course.

Tulip, delighted to have her original owners back, laid her head on Mike's knee and looked at him with pure adoration. Perhaps I hadn't paid as much attention to her as I could have.

"Forgot how beautiful it was in Michigan," Uncle Mike said.

Not what I thought he was going to say.

"Trees changed colors, the lake water was such a deep blue. Big hearty trees, not like the scrubby pines down here." He shook his head. "Took me back to when I was a kid. Even saw a few early snowflakes."

Carol nodded. I waited. I thought they'd run back to Florida as fast as they could, escaping the north before winter settled in.

"I'll just say it," Carol said. "Savvy, my crazy mother needs a full-time keeper, but she won't move down here."

Oh, shit. They wanted me to do crazy Aunt Gwen duty? I hadn't told them I wanted to stay here in Barefoot Key, and I had no idea what they were planning.

"Do you need my help?" I asked neutrally, wanting to be a champion niece but hoping they would say no.

"Do we ever," Mike said emphatically. "How would you feel about scrapping your Chicago job and taking over for us permanently?"

"With Aunt Gwen?"

Carol and Mike stared at me and then burst out laughing. Carol shook her head. "I wouldn't wish that old bat on anyone."

"We mean here," Mike said. "The Gull. If you'll take it off our hands. We want to move home. Retire north instead of south like normal people."

"Take over The Gull?"

"Take it," Carol said. "The whole thing. You can have it."

"Have it?"

Fighting for understanding, I glanced over at Skip's bar. He was shirtless, sweeping off the sand from the beach entrance. He caught my eye, waved, and started over. Maybe I looked desperate.

"It's all yours," Mike reiterated. "We want to give it to you, no strings attached."

"But...you can't just give away a motel," I protested.

"Sure we can. It's ours. We paid it off years ago and put away money to retire on. Don't need to buy a house since we'll have to be on site with Gwen to keep her on the sunny side of the law. Really," he said. "We want to give it to you."

I glanced around The Gull, seeing it with fresh eyes. What if it were mine?

"We were planning to leave it to you when we kicked the bucket anyway," Carol said. "But that's silly. Why not transfer it now when you can really make something out of it?"

Skip stepped onto the concrete patio and accepted a shameless display of affection from Tulip before pulling up a chair touching mine.

"Looks like I missed something big," he observed.

"We're giving Savvy The Gull. Retiring north to take care of Carol's mother," Mike said.

Skip's eyebrows flew up, and he turned a shocked face to mine.

"Really," I said.

"The place looks better than ever. You've done a great job running it, even though you were busy rescuing the whole town," Carol said, smiling. "And I love your new look," she added, indicating my outfit and bare feet. A far cry from my former buttoned and covered up state.

"I didn't exactly save the whole town," I said.

"Not what we heard. And we heard *a lot* at the party last night," Mike said.

"People were doing a lot of drinking, but it's true. Savvy isn't just another pretty face," Skip agreed. "She figured out the scheme and flushed out the swindlers."

Maria's cleaning cart rolled nearby and she paused, leaning on it and watching our little group under a patio umbrella. Carol scooted her chair closer to mine. "What do you think, honey? Are you happy here? You sure look it to me, but this has to be your decision. Do you want to stay in Barefoot and put down some Florida roots?"

I smiled. "Skip asked me the same thing this morning."

Carol's expectant look magnified. "Skip asked you a question, did he?"

277

"I knew it!" Maria exclaimed. "Just like in my dream."

"And I said yes. Looks like staying in Barefoot Key is the savvy thing for me to do," I said.

Skip slipped an arm around me, my aunt and uncle raised a glass, and Tulip settled happily on my bare toes in the sunshine.

The End

About Amie Denman

Amie Denman lives in a small town in her native Ohio with her husband and sons. When she's not reading or writing, she enjoys walking and running outside. The owner of a powerful case of curiosity, she's been known to chase fire trucks on her bicycle just to see what's going on. Amie believes that everything is fun: especially roller coasters, wedding cake, and falling in love. For more information, please visit www.amiedenman.com

###

Made in the USA
Lexington, KY
17 June 2016